All he wanted was not to let his Captain down.

"There is one known to me," the Captain continued with saddened eyes, "whose need is desperate. His heart longs for everything Evermore has and is. But because he lives where the Pretender claims rule, he is deceived, and thinks Evermore is a lying dream."

Denemir slipped from the stone seat and knelt. "I go wherever you send me, liege."

The Captain's blue eyes looked deep into Denemir. For many seconds, the only sound was the foaming water outside. The Captain answered, "Your heart is right, but you have little experience. Such a journey could cost your life. I release you to stay here if you wish. I will not think less of you."

The young knight returned the Captain's gaze. "If you tell me to go," he said, "then I know there must be a way I can succeed."

Little did he know what lie ahead...

KNIGHTS OF EVERMORE

KNIGHTS OF EVERMORE

SCOTT & RENEE PINZON

bethel
publishing
1819 S. Main
Elkhart, IN 46516

Published by
Bethel Publishing Company
1819 South Main Street
Elkhart, Indiana 46516

Cover illustration by Craig Kosak
Design and Logotype by James Clark Design Images
Art Direction and Typesetting by Scott Pinzon

Printed and Bound in the United States of America

ISBN # 0–934998–56–6

Dedication

For Dad, who got the ball rolling not only on this project,
but also long ago when he first said,
"You can be anything you want
if you put your mind to it, son!"

Table of Contents

Acknowledgments

Musicians get to thank a hundred people on the liner notes of their tapes and CDs, so why can't authors?

The Pinzons wish to express heartfelt affection and thanks to Grant and Lisa Crawford, for being sent by the High King to offer special aid and rescue during our discouraging stay at an outpost in Ssenkrad.

Thanks to all the sentries who watched for us back in Evermore, especially Chuck ("the Bop"), Kathy, Abigail, and Joshua Gould. An extra clank of weaponry and a salute go to the Haynes. Surprise! We wrote two chapters of this book in your basement!

Lessons in this manuscript might not have been learned, and the ending would have been decidedly different, without the shining examples of Frank and Laurie Ascanio and Kelly and Merrilyn Carpenter. All four of you are clueless—about how to stop loving.

For invaluable intercessory support, we thank our unforgettable Head Grump, Sylvia Copp, who pointed out the difference between a path and a valley.

Preface

This is one of those fussy introductions by the author, and if such trivia bores you, feel free to skip right to the story. But if you enjoy getting a small "behind-the-scenes" peek at the origin of a book, then this is for you.

Several years ago, I wrote a story called "The Rebel and the Point of the Sword" for a church newsletter. As often happens in the mysterious but rarely boring world of donation-based budgeting, the newsletter never got published. About that time a magazine called *TQ* asked to run my first novel, *Splendini!*, as a 12-part serial.

What's a *TQ*, I wondered. Teetotaler's Quarterly? Tentative Quitters? Totally Qool? *TQ* turned out to be the nickname of *Teen Quest*, a magazine known previously as *Young Ambassador*.

Since the story I had written had no home, on a whim I sent it to *TQ*. They liked it. They published it. And, short as it was, it drew letters. A pastor from Pennsylvania requested permission to reprint the story in his church bulletin. Comments and letters from other *TQ* readers showed a surprisingly enthusiastic reception.

I sent *TQ* an outline of four more stories about Gulliver Lamm, the good-hearted but error-prone aspiring knight.

TQ ran those stories, and again the mail came. In letter after letter, readers—especially teens and young adults—said they had grown closer to God while relating to Gulliver's misadventures.

Over the years, I kept sending the stories. Most of them benefited because my wife Renee reviewed them in their early stages. Many times I forced her to drop what she was doing because I was excited about a stack of pages fresh off the laser printer. Her honesty sometimes deflated me, but her input always improved the work and encouraged me not to settle for mediocrity. Eventually, her input became so valuable that it was only fair to add her name to the by-line. By the time Gulliver became Denemir (pronounced DEN-uh-meer), Renee wasn't merely responding to drafts of written stories. She was plotting the stories with me during long walks among the towering pines and rustic stables of the Pacific Northwest. This fact often amazes new acquaintances, one of whom exclaimed, "You two plot *together?* I thought husbands and wives were supposed to plot *against* each other!"

It is now seven years and seventeen installments since the first Evermore story appeared in *TQ*. The stories are all collected here for the first time. (A limited-circulation mail order book published by Back to the Bible in 1992, *Tales of Evermore*, contained the first eight stories.) Because Renee and I thought each Evermore story might be the last one, the world of Evermore grew in fits and starts, without the benefit of a previously worked out master plan. We wrote the stories to strict word counts and often under aggressive deadlines. In that sense, we see places where the stories could be improved. Yet we keep hearing from enthused teens, parents, teachers, and pastors who convince us these little parables have a life of their own.

Now we offer them to you, encouraging you to read them with eyes that see and ears that hear. The story of Gulliver and his fellow knights, we can tell you. But the story of the High King and the Captain of the Guard, and their feelings about a knight living at your house—well, you'll have to hear *that* story from your own heart.

Scott Pinzon
Seattle
Valentine's Day, 1994

1

The King's One True Sign

TRUDGING WEARILY through the woods at the end of an uneventful patrol, Gulliver Lamm didn't notice, high in the oaks, the birdsong that greeted the pink and orange clouds of sunset. Lost in thought, the lanky young foot soldier stared only at the dirt as he marched. He heaved a dejected sigh.

If only.

If only he were a full-fledged knight instead of a foot soldier, he wouldn't be dragging his sore feet home to the castle right now. He would be mounted on a proud, well-trained battle horse. If only he were a full-fledged knight, this heavy sword wouldn't be threatening to fall from his narrow hips at each step, forcing him to hike his sword-belt up every few minutes. It would be sheathed in a case attached to his saddle, leaving his legs free. If only he were a full-fledged knight, he would be educated by royal tutors instead of gaining experience the hard way—on solitary patrol.

As Gulliver walked, he found himself on the edge of the

river that fed into the castle's moat a mile away. Absently, he began following the river bank toward home and resumed his thoughts.

Most of all, if only he were a knight instead of a foot soldier, he could wear the sign of the King. Each knight wore a tabard, a sleeveless shirt that was nothing more than a front and back panel with a head hole, over their armor. Knights commanded instant respect all over the kingdom because on their tabards, heraldic symbols declared in bold colors that they fought for the High King. Gulliver frowned at the thought of his boring chain mail vest, and the leather helm he wore instead of a shining steel helmet. He would skip the horse, the tutor, and all the rest if only he could wear the sign of the King whom he loved so much.

A sound interrupted Gulliver's thoughts. He froze in place, suddenly alert, listening. His hand gripped the pommel of his sword.

The breeze changed and the sound came again, carried faintly in the air. Young voices, maybe children, shouting. He lifted his head, straining to hear. It was one word, over and over, coming from upstream: *"He-e-e-lp!"*

The young soldier charged upstream, in the direction of the castle, leaping over stones and shrubs. His leather boots slipped on the slick rocks near the river bank, nearly plunging him headlong, but he kept running as fast as he could.

The river curved, becoming wider than a street, slicing through a thick stand of oaks. Rushing toward the cries, Gulliver rounded the bend and burst upon the scene.

His eyes drank it in rapidly. In the middle of the river drifted a long, light boat pointed at both ends, a craft that Gulliver knew as a wherry. In the wherry were four small children and a blonde peasant girl who had probably seen fourteen or fifteen summers. As the boat rotated in an aimless circle, the soldier spied a length of frayed rope dangling over the gunnel into the water. The children cried while the girl yelled for help. None of them had seem him yet.

At first he puzzled at their distress. Then, across the river, he saw more of the story: a crude dock; a pair of oars on the dock; and, tied to the dock, another worn piece of rope like the one drooping from the wherry. The children must have been playing in the moored boat when the old rope tore. Now they were about to drift into the center of the river, where the current would grab the boat and speed it all the way to the rapids. If they survived the rocks of the white water, they would not survive the Great Falls.

Gulliver scampered along the water's edge, pacing the wherry. He tried to see how deep the river was. If it was shallow, he should leave his chain mail and boots on so that he would be heavy enough to walk to the boat. If it was deep, he should remove everything he could so that he could swim unhindered.

Scrambling sideways, he heard the knight before seeing him. Rapid hoofbeats pounded to a halt behind him. By the time Gulliver had spun around, a knight twice as tall as the young soldier had leapt off a black stallion to the ground. The knight's tabard bore shepherd's staves crossed below a golden crown, on a field of purple.

Gulliver thumped his right fist against his heart, the combat salute of the King's soldiers. He began, "I'm glad you are here, Sire—"

The knight brushed past him without a glance, stopped at the water's edge, and stared at the wherry. In a flash he grasped the situation. He shouted to the children, "Ho! Over here! I shall rescue you, in the name of the King! *Hallo!*"

The armored knight continued calling until the children in the boat finally saw him. The three smallest ones jumped to their feet to beg for help. The boat immediately overturned, throwing all its occupants into the icy water.

Gulliver cried out in fear. With anxious eyes, he watched as the maiden's head broke the surface and she clung to the boat bottom, which now faced the sky. Two more heads appeared . . . three . . . where was the last child? There! Now all five of them clung to the capsized wherry, four of them wailing.

As the knight set one foot in the water, more hooves thundered up behind Gulliver. He turned to see a second huge knight jump from a fully-dressed battle horse. This knight's tabard and shield both depicted a blue Star of David surrounding a lion rampant upon a field of white. "Hold there, knight!" the second knight cried. "I must perform this rescue, for the greater glory of the King!"

The first knight turned to survey the newcomer. "You cannot! That is not the King's true token you bear! I will rescue these children, that the King may get glory!"

The second knight unsheathed a sword from his saddle and stomped up to the first knight. "You know not what you say, Sir! I bear the symbol of the Lion of the tribe of Judah! That is the ancestry of the King! This is his one true sign!"

Gulliver watched in frustration. Court etiquette did not permit a foot soldier to intervene with anything when a knight was present, much less two knights. He stared worriedly at the children. As one slipped beneath the surface, only to be recovered by the peasant girl, the first knight countered, "And I wear the sign of both shepherd and royalty, which are both callings of the King! Now stand back, lest you get splashed—"

"I can prove I am from the King and you are not," the second knight interrupted. "Behold my sword, and it's inscription!"

"It is the same as mine, and thus no better—"

"Nay! See here? The words originally spoken by the Captain of the Guard himself are inscribed in blood red! Your sword's inscription is plain!"

Gulliver mustered all his courage. "Please, kind Sires! Both of you bear signs I have seen the King use! The important thing is the drowning children—"

"Bah! Color! Do you know what the inscription says? Somehow I doubt it!"

"Know what it says? I know it full well and I know how to *use* it, too! Defend yourself, Sir Knight!"

More hooves pounded to a halt. A third knight dismounted. He carried a lance with a pennant on the end of it. The pennant showed a white heart with two red drops emblazoned on a field of black. "Stay your hand, gentlemen!" he called. "I serve the High King, and I will rescue yon children in His name!"

Gulliver groaned. The boat had floated into the middle of the stream. Suddenly the powerful current seized the wherry. It quit spinning and began to head down river, slowly increasing speed. If only court custom did not forbid him from acting!

"You are both impostors!"

"That is not the King's standard!"

"I'll settle this now! Tell me what oath you took when you entered the King's service—*if* you ever entered the King's service!"

"I owe you no explanation! Ask him yourself next time you see him—*if* you've ever seen him!"

Anxiety grew in Gulliver. Now one of the little boys was no longer holding onto the boat. With numb fingers, he tried to cling to the length of worn rope trailing behind the wherry. His hands were slipping. Gulliver danced in frustration and hollered at the knights, "One of you or all of you, it matters not! *Someone* do the deed!"

"But only people who match my standard truly serve the King!"

"Nay! Your standard does not matter, because only I have the *King's* standard!"

He could wait no longer, no matter how much trouble he would be in. Gulliver sprinted downstream as the children screamed. Running hard, he slowly caught up with the boat and passed it. As soon as he estimated that he was far enough ahead of the boat to intercept it, he dashed into the chilling water, frantically hoping it wouldn't go over his head.

When the water reached his heaving chest, the young soldier felt the current begin to tug at him. Planting his feet wide apart in the muddy bottom, he leaned into the current and waited for the boat. Dimly he noted the clank and ring of sword blows on armor coming from the knights on shore.

Then there was no time to think. The boat rushed toward him. He twisted to one side and gripped its edge with all his strength. He tried to dig his heels into the river bottom, but the wherry's momentum dragged him several steps downstream. Straining every muscle in his body, he pulled on the boat and managed to drag it halfway out of the current. The current pushed the rear of the boat faster than the front, where he clung grimly, and the boat moved in a circle. Suddenly it was in front of Gulliver, dragging him along.

Again Gulliver tried to plant himself and halt the progress of the boat. The peasant girl, realizing what he was doing, also dragged her feet. Together they slowed the boat enough that the force of the current threw the boat to one side, slowing it drastically. Within moments it was in the shallows where even the smallest child could wade.

Using his last burst of strength, Gulliver hauled the boat halfway onto the shore and dropped it in the mud. He helped everyone flounder up the embankment to a grassy clearing, where they all collapsed in a soggy heap, gasping for air.

After a minute the maiden was able to gasp, "Thank you . . . kind Sire, for . . . saving us!"

Gulliver rolled over on his side so he could see her. Shaking wet brown hair out of his eyes, he panted, "My pleasure!"

The girl sat up and took the smallest child in her arms, comforting it with small noises. Then she glanced at the young soldier and said, "Why wouldn't those other knights help you? 'Twas almost more than one could do!"

"They were arguing," Gulliver admitted. "About who wore the one true sign of the King."

Despite her soaked clothes, the girl laughed merrily. The children, though not understanding, grinned at the sound. "Why, you're the only one who shows the sign of the King!"

Gulliver rose to his feet. He looked his dripping self over in surprise. Finally he replied, "I wear no tabard, no shield or pennon, maiden! How did you even know I serve the King?"

Sharing his surprise, the maiden stared back. "I know not what fancy learning you receive in the royal court," she said. "I know they have many complicated customs there. But among us commoners the King's only true sign is well known. Do they not know in the castle that the sign of the King is love?"

For a moment, Gulliver was speechless. Then he collapsed in the grass and laughed heartily at himself.

At length he told the peasant girl, "It is I who must thank you. I had forgotten that the King's servant is not measured by what is on his shield but by what is in his heart. I dare say you are a King's servant, too."

In agreement, they both smiled. At that instant Gulliver knew that he would not trade the feeling of this soaking wet moment on the grassy bank for all the knightly standards and emblems in the world.

The Eyes of the King

HERE WAS the ten feet of moat that the work detail had widened, as the King had commanded. And yonder was the thousand feet of moat left to go.

Hip-deep in moat muck, Gulliver Lamm paused to smear his sweaty forehead against the shoulder of his equally sweaty jerkin. Between ragged gasps, he glanced skyward. With dismay he saw that the summer sun had barely peaked. It was just after the midday repast, but he felt as though he had worked an entire day, or perhaps two. His weak knees nearly buckled as he hauled another shovelful of mud to shore.

On the inside shore of the moat, leaning back in the cool shade of the castle walls, sprawled the remainder of the work detail. All nine of them were young foot soldiers like Gulliver. As he glanced wearily at them, a dark-haired soldier wearing a man-styled blouse open to the waist called to him, "Persevere, friend! I feel the moat trembling at your furious onslaught!"

Another soldier, lying in a clump of clover, responded,

"At least he does not think the moat will widen itself, as our friend Luke Warrem seems to!" The other soldiers laughed at Luke, the dark-haired soldier.

In mock humility, Luke replied, "I beg thy mercy. Only a bit more rest for my weary bones, and I will widen the moat myself." More sarcastic laughter followed the comment. Luke grinned as if accepting applause, then idly lobbed a dirt clod at a napping friend's nose.

Refusing to groan or sigh, Gulliver tightened his blistered hands on his shovel and dumped its contents on the lawn. He waded deeper into the moat and plunged the shovel into the mire near his feet. The stirred mud had turned the water an opaque golden brown. But when the shovel felt full, he hauled it to the surface and began slogging toward the other shore, away from the soldiers, where he could dump it out for the millionth time. It was but ten short steps, yet he was so tired the trip gave him time to think back on the start of the day . . .

Dawn. The task force worked hard at first. In one hour they had made a noticeable gouge in the existing moat. Luke, claiming he had gotten mud in his eye, sat down for a quick break. The others, including Gulliver, rested too.

By ten o' the clock the gouge had hardly doubled in length, but the detail headed for a third break. The second had been so long that their clothes had dried. The idea of resting three times before lunch didn't strike Gulliver as being right, so he worked through the third break. Luke immediately singled him out for ridicule, which surprised Gulliver;

he was only doing what he thought was right.

No one else showed any signs of getting up again until moments before the regularly scheduled patrol passed by. When the knights cantered past, all ten soldiers were up to their waist in the moat, digging hard. The moment the knights passed from sight, Gulliver was alone in the water again.

Astonished at the brazen deceit and laziness of his brother soldiers, he challenged the one who acted as if he were their leader—Luke.

But Luke neatly turned the group against Gulliver. "Don't you see that you are ruining it for all of us?"

Gulliver was dumbfounded. *"What?"*

"Of course!" Luke insisted. "You see, this job is much too large. It will take the ten of us at least two fortnights to broaden this soggy trench. Soon the King will realize that. The slower we go, the sooner he will give us help."

Gulliver cast a calculating eye upon Luke. "Thus by obeying the King, I am 'ruining things.' This is strange logic indeed!"

Luke winked playfully. "Look about you, man! We are at the rear of the citadel. The only entrance is at the front. No one comes here but the patrols, whose schedules I know. We are so close to the walls that not even the sentries in the battlements can see us. We can dig a little and play a lot. There are worse ways to spend a summer!"

"Yes, such as in the dungeon, serving penitence for dereliction of duty!"

"We are safe, Gulliver! Rest with us! What say ye?"

The young soldier bent to pick up his shovel. His back hurt when he bent, and his blistered hand protested against the wooden handle. When he straightened, he fixed Luke with a steady gaze. "I say, the eyes of the King see." Luke looked disgusted, but Gulliver persisted with his warning. "'Tis written on each of our swords: 'The eyes of our King search to and fro throughout the earth, that He might find the one whose heart is completely His.'" Gulliver paused awkwardly. "There is more to the saying, but . . . I cannot remember it right now."

Luke let out a hiss of breath and gave the other soldiers a look as if to say, *How can one reason with a fool like this?* Then he demanded, "How can the King see us from inside a palace of stone?"

Gulliver had no answer. "The eyes of the King see," he repeated. He walked further into the moat and resumed digging.

The rest of the day went the same. Some of the soldiers lolled against the castle wall; others played at quarter staves with their shovels. One sunbathed; another dozed. But each time a knight or an officer passed by on their rounds, they saw the task force working hard in the moat.

As the hours passed, Gulliver wanted more and more to collapse on the grass with his fellows. But he was sure that, somehow, the King would learn about the laziness of the others. "The eyes of the King see!" His Highness would surely know; and knowing, would dispense discipline . . .

Gulliver's reverie ended. He bounced the side of his

shovel blade on the grass to knock the mud out.

Behind him, there abruptly began a furious churning and splashing. He turned in time to see soldiers plunging and flopping into the water. They swam across the deep area and surfaced all around him, rising to their feet in the new, shallower portion of the moat, clutching shovels. Before the water quit running off their hair and faces, the detail had dredged up heavy clumps of mud and water weed and proceeded to wade toward the shore.

Suddenly, from out of the forest, a trio of horns sounded a clear, bright fanfare in the summer air. An answering trumpet echoed from a sentry high atop the castle. A column of knights galloped into sight, colorful pennons flying from uplifted lances. As they thundered into view, their armor flashed in the sunlight, searing Gulliver's eyes.

Two score of knights formed two straight rows that led from the forest, through the clearing, and past the moat. At the far end of the rows, another group of knights appeared from the forest, escorting a red velvet coach drawn by seven horses wearing golden battle dress.

The foot soldiers in the moat stopped bantering and exchanged glances. Visiting nobility! Everyone dug faster—except Gulliver, who was already digging his pitiful fastest.

The coach drove between the two rows of mounted knights. Another fanfare sounded, this time a lengthy one from the castle walls. This was an imposing visitor indeed.

The coach was passing mere feet from the moat when it halted.

A knight whose ostrich feathers atop his helmet denoted his high rank rode up beside the coach and addressed a person inside. "A problem, milord?"

Gulliver speared the bottom with his shovel, then glanced at the coach. An overweight man wearing an avalanche of ruffles at his throat peered out of the coach's window. "Merely curious, my good knight. What are those servants doing in the moat?"

"Those are foot soldiers, milord. They are widening the moat so that attackers will have difficulty crossing it."

"Ah. I see." The man continued watching.

In silence, the young soldiers labored at looking competent. The summer sun bore down, but not as hot upon them as the gaze of royalty.

Finally the man murmured something to the knight. "Even your foot soldiers are admirably industrious, all except that slow one. In my kingdom, we have such laggards whipped."

Briefly, Gulliver's eyes met those of the man in the coach. A thrill of embarrassment rushed through him. He tried to push himself more quickly. Instead he tripped in knee-deep water and splatted headlong in the shallows. Panicking, he tried to scramble to his feet, but the shovel handle tangled between his legs. Down he went again.

Gulliver gasped for breath as he rose to all fours. He expected boisterous laughter. But it was worse than that.

Everyone was silent. Staring.

Finally, the coach moved on. The mounted escort's jingle-rustle-thud followed after it. By the time Gulliver had stood and wiped the water from his eyes, the two columns of knights were folding in upon themselves and following after the coach. Many of the knights wagged their heads as they passed.

Because the columns of the honor guard were still in sight, Luke kept working. But as he carried a load past Gulliver, he said, "If the eyes of the King see as much as you say—I will visit you in prison."

Gulliver alternately fought the desire to yell obscenities and the urge to weep.

Twenty silent, back-straining shovelfuls later, another coach had arrived at the moat. This was the black metal one used for transporting prisoners to trial. The huge driver, also attired in black, pointed the handle of his whip at Gulliver. "You! Inside."

He released his shovel right where he stood. The handle made a quiet *bloop* as it disappeared under water. He dragged himself to the dark coach, wondering if he would drop out of sight just as completely.

The driver in black had climbed down from his seat and opened the rear door for him. After the forlorn soldier climbed in, the door creaked and banged shut behind him, leaving him in almost complete darkness. He stumbled against a narrow bench that ran along the side of the coach and collapsed onto it. He slumped in shame and covered his face with both hands. The coach lurched into motion.

"Be not afraid."

Gulliver's head jerked up. It had not occurred to him that another prisoner might be hidden in the darkness. "Who goes there?"

"'Tis I, Gulliver. Be anxious for nothing."

He knew that voice. It was . . . no, this couldn't be! It was the Captain of the Guard—the King's only son! "Sire," Gulliver breathed, "surely they cannot arrest you!"

The Captain's laugh actually seemed to bring light into the dark coach. "No, Gulliver. I am lord over this wagon. It is not used only for prisoners. I sometimes use the trial coach for privacy, to shut my faithful servants in with me while we talk. Servants such as you."

"Faithful servants? I . . ."

"The King's high tower easily oversees all that the soldiers do. We saw your solitary devotion and sent this coach to rescue you."

"But I embarrassed your kingdom—"

"The eyes of the King do *truly* see, young one. You thought He would see only the wrong. But he saw it all. He saw your heart." A tone of command crept into the voice in the gloom. "Therefore kneel, soldier."

Gulliver threw himself to his knees, heart pumping air. A strong hand placed itself gently upon the crown of his head.

"No more are you merely a foot soldier. I christen you now a Squire and a novice Knight in Training. Continue faithful, and you will one day be a knight of the kingdom, answerable only to me. Rise, Squire Lamm."

Gulliver rose shakily. This was nearly too much. "But, what of the others? They—"

"What is that to thee? Follow thou me! Your King, who sees in secret, shall reward you openly."

Less than a week later, Gulliver and a few other loyal foot soldiers were brought before the King in pomp and glory to be officially anointed Squires. A crowd filled the royal chapel, far larger than the group that had seen Gulliver's shame. Head held high, Gulliver slowly strode toward the throne, up the stone aisle that flower bearers had strewn with rose petals. He wore a fine scarlet cloak that the Captain had given him. A choir sang powerfully:

> *"The eyes of our King search to and fro*
> *Throughout the earth, that He might find the ones*
> *Whose hearts are completely His,*
> *Whose hearts are completely His,"*

And with a rush of joyous tears, Gulliver remembered the next line, which he had forgotten in the moat. As he approached the King, he joined in singing,

> *". . . That He might fully support them!"*

3

The Point of the Sword

I T HAD been only a week since Gulliver Lamm's promotion to Squire, but that was the farthest thing from his mind at the moment.

Chain mail flashing in the sunlight, he scrambled along the mossy rocks in desperate pursuit of the rebel. The dark-headed man had disappeared around a bend in the gully, but a grim smile played at Gulliver's lips. Other soldiers had spent months chasing this man. But Gulliver knew what lay around the gully's bend. He had the rebel cornered.

Gulliver paused to unsheathe his sword. The tempered steel rang as it slid from the scabbard. Beautiful inscriptions covered the blade, and gems encrusted the hilt. The soldier gripped it firmly and stepped around one last boulder.

Breathing heavily, the man crouched with his back to a cliff and glared at Gulliver. "So," he snarled. "Finally you have trapped me. What do you intend?"

Gulliver stepped closer. "I instruct you to cease your rebellious ways and surrender unconditionally to the King. Your fate will depend on his mercy."

The man sneered. "And if I refuse?"

The young soldier reached out with his sword and slit the laces of the rebel's jerkin. "If you refuse," he said, placing the gleaming sword point against the man's bare chest, "I will put the question to you again after my sword pierces your heart."

The man shrank back against the stone, staring at the razor-sharp point. Suddenly he startled Gulliver Lamm by bursting into laughter.

"What ails you, knave?" Gulliver demanded. "Why do you laugh so?"

The man wiped a tear of mirth from his eyes. "Forgive me, young soldier. The very idea that that useless trifle in your hands could pierce me strikes me as quite amusing."

"This is no ordinary sword," Gulliver threatened. "It is an everlasting sword, fashioned by the King himself."

The man nearly collapsed in gales of laughter. Finally he managed, "Who—who told you that?"

Gulliver was taken aback. "Why—the sword itself says so!"

"It does not," the stranger stated. "Show me."

The point swung away from the rebel's heart as Gulliver turned it sideways to read part of the inscription. "Hearken," he said, and read aloud, "This sword is living and active, sharper than any double-edged sword, penetrating even to the dividing of soul and spirit, joints and marrow; it judges the thoughts and attitude of the heart.' There, you see?"

The rebel seemed unimpressed. "Of course the sword

would say that about itself," he countered. "You reason in a circle. You say, 'If you don't believe in the sword, just ask the sword.' You have no proof!"

"But this same sword pierces me!" Gulliver said, confusion clouding his mind. "I know it works!"

"Faugh!" the man said. "That is you. I am me. That makes all the difference. Besides, I have talked to others who bear a sword like yours and they all disagree. No one knows how that sword really works."

Now the blade drooped from Gulliver's hand to the ground. "What do you mean?" he asked.

"Well," the man said confidently, "learned men of the realm have proven that the inscriptions on the sword contain grievous errors and the sayings contradict each other. The sword was not actually fashioned by the King—whom I have never seen, I might add—but by simple men such as yourself who sought to explain what no man can understand."

All thought of fighting had left Gulliver. Sweat trickled down from under his helmet. "But I know it works—"

Without warning, the rebel hurled a stone from behind his back and dealt a tremendous blow to Gulliver's head. The King's soldier staggered back a step, off balance. The man placed his hands on Gulliver's shoulders and pushed him down, then leaped over the flailing warrior and darted away. Before Gulliver could lift his armored form back to its feet, the man had made it to the cliffs high above.

The rebel shouted a taunt back at Gulliver. "You had me,

my friend!" he called. "Almost! But I tricked you!" His mocking laugh echoed down to Gulliver. "What kind of fool defends his weapon when he should *use* it?" And the man was gone.

Shamed, Gulliver stared at the spot where the man had stood. The chase could have ended today, but now it would drag on. The King would forgive Gulliver readily enough, but the rebel's question haunted him.

"Indeed," Gulliver murmured. He sheathed his sword and once again trudged after the rebel. "What kind of fool?"

A Dark and Stormy Knight

HIGH ATOP the battlements on the castle towers, sentries tugged their cloaks more closely about them as the storm winds grew. Above, black clouds billowed like an army surging across the leaden sky toward the citadel.

The scuffle and ring of boots pounding on flagstone echoed in the outermost courtyard. A detail of knights and foot soldiers, hastily summoned, hurried into formation.

Lanky Gulliver Lamm leapt down a final flight of stairs, scarlet cloak flying behind him. He dashed across the courtyard and found his place at the rear of the ranks. Breathless, he asked the more experienced soldier next to him, "What causes the alarm?"

In reply, the bearded soldier jerked his head toward the sky.

Gulliver stared at the looming thunderclouds, and could not find the sun anywhere.

He looked back at the soldier. "How long 'til yonder storm breaks?"

"No man knows," the soldier admitted. "There has never been a storm such as this." As if to prove his words, distant thunder rumbled low and long.

A page shouted, "The Captain of the Guard!" The foot soldiers snapped to attention. The knights dropped to one knee, heads bowed.

A white steed bearing a tall man, deep-chested and strong of arm, cantered across the courtyard and halted directly in front of the task force. The man's beard and flowing hair were black with white streaks. Over his breastplate he wore a blue jersey displaying three golden lions rampant. Like the knights and soldiers, he had a silver sword in a golden scabbard strapped to his waist. In a deep voice, he commanded, "Rise!"

The knights stood.

The Captain's voice conveyed authority without arrogance. "I thank you for hastening to answer the alarm," he boomed over the moaning wind. "You know of the approaching storm. But your eyes have not seen what the lookouts have seen."

The sky grew noticeably darker as more clouds piled up overhead. The Captain glanced up, then spoke faster. "With lightning and torrents of rain, this storm devastates all in its path. Its wind is fierce enough to uproot tall trees. It removes everything that can be shaken, that only those things which cannot be shaken may remain."

Nervously, Gulliver clenched and unclenched his sword handle as it hung by his side. Wind pulled at the rose hedges in the courtyard and tore the petals from the flowers. They brushed across Gulliver's face as the Captain continued.

"The storm will cross directly over the land of Evermore. Our villagers and townspeople will lose everything. But no matter how fierce the gale, it cannot shake the King's City, which is built on solid rock! The townspeople need not lose their lives if we can compel them to come inside the walls!"

A flash of lightning lit the scene briefly. Startled, the Captain's horse skittered to one side. "Many of the townspeople do not know the one entrance to the City!" the Captain shouted over the wind. "If they do not find it, they will die. Your mission is to ride forth and warn everyone you can. If necessary, escort them to the entrance. And mark ye, it is the last hour before darkness falls. Work hard while it is yet daylight, men!" With that, a clap of thunder finally followed the lightning.

"Above all, remember this," he finished. "The King is not willing that any should perish!" The Captain of the Guard drew his sword and lifted it in the air. He paused, gazing upon the men, his steely eyes driving the message home. Then, as if cutting them loose, the sword flashed down. "Now *go!*"

With a shout, the men ran from the courtyard. Just outside it, a row of fresh horses in battle dress awaited. Within moments the force had mounted and galloped away.

Gulliver found himself riding a sorrel mare. Most of the knights had rushed toward town. The novice soldier decided to strike out toward the farms instead, that no one would be overlooked.

He followed a path through the woods where the deepening gloom renewed his sense of haste. He dug his heels into the horse's flanks, urging it to its greatest speed.

Soon he came upon the borders of a small farm. In the field, a short, grumpy-looking peasant trudged behind an ox and plow. Gulliver pulled up and called, "Ho, friend! I bear tidings from the King!"

The balding peasant kept plowing. Eventually he replied with disdain, "That cannot be, for I have never met the King."

"But the King knows you," Gulliver declared. "He offers to you the safety of his citadel, to preserve you from the great and terrible storm that approaches even now!"

At that, the peasant clicked his mouth twice and the ox stopped. The man gazed long and hard into the sky. He gazed equally long and hard at Gulliver. Finally he said, "Afraid of rain? My crops long for water, and I, sir, do not melt." He resumed plowing.

Gulliver trotted the horse to keep pace with the ox. "But you do not understand! There has never been a storm like this. Nothing can stand before it."

"Begone, knave. I'm busy."

A blaze of lightning turned the world bright white for half a second. Gulliver pushed away his irritation at being called 'knave' and said, "You see? This is no mere smattering of drops! You are in danger! Gather your family and come!" Then the thunder exploded overhead. Gulliver's horse whinnied and reared, nearly throwing him. The storm had moved closer by miles since the Captain gave his command. Louder, Gulliver insisted, "You say you are busy, yet you tend a crop that will be destroyed before dawn!"

The plower stopped. He turned to Gulliver. "If it's so dangerous," the farmer said with a sneer, "what are you doing out here, varlet?"

Indignation rose in Gulliver. "Trying to help *you!*"

"Yes, and you want me to believe this comes from the goodness of your heart. Oh," he added sarcastically, "and of course, the King's, who has never met me." He put his hands on his hips and stared defiantly at Gulliver.

By now the gale blew so strong that the crops lay down before it. The peasant shouted to be heard. "I see through you, knave. You would escort me only as far as the wood where no one sees, and rob me of all my money. No, thank you. Some other day, mayhap." The man tried to resume plowing, but the frightened ox only laid its ears back and stood firm.

Gulliver was beside himself. "Why, you dull-witted, base—" Just then an awful peal of thunder and lightning covered his words.

"So!" the peasant yelled gleefully. "You insult me! I knew your kindness was nothing more than a pose! Why should I enter the King's City when it is *filled* with you hypocrites?"

The first fat drops of rain nearly steamed as they hit the face of the fuming soldier. His sword rang as it leaped from its sheath. "Churlish ingrate," he growled through clenched teeth, "I will save you if it is the last thing I do!"

Now the dull peasant understood danger. He yelped and scurried away.

In a trice, Gulliver ran him down. With a mighty wallop from the flat of his sword, Gulliver knocked the farmer over.

The soldier dropped from his mount. The peasant came up fighting, trying to kick Gulliver. The squire caught the man's foot at the end of its swing and yanked on it, again tumbling the peasant to the loam.

Gulliver rested his sword's gleaming point at the man's throat. "To your feet!" he barked.

Glaring balefully at the young soldier, the farmer rose to all fours. Brusquely Gulliver grabbed him by the back of his jerkin and trousers, flung him stomach down across the horse's withers, and leaped into the saddle. At the touch of the soldier's heels, the horse sprang forward.

"Help!" cried the farmer. "Robber! Kidnapper! Thief!" And, as the horse jounced through a pothole, "Uulph!"

"Silence!" Gulliver cried, sheathing his sword as the horse ran. "I am saving your miserable life! Were it left to me, I would let you perish for your insolence! But lucky for you, that is not mine to decide."

"It is *mine,*" the farmer fairly screamed. "You can't do this to me! It is *my* life!"

A burst of wind, heavy with rain, flailed at them and passed on. The wind now howled too loudly for Gulliver to reply. The battle horse flew as if running for its very life.

Soon, ducking evergreen branches in the twilight, Gulliver could just make out the gate of the City rushing toward them. The horse thundered up to the entrance, its hooves throwing mud as Gulliver reined to a halt.

He jumped off and hauled on the peasant's legs until the farmer spilled to the ground. Instantly the peasant tried to run away. Gulliver grabbed one arm, but the farmer brought the other arm around and tried to bash Gulliver's face. Instead, both of them slipped and fell in a writhing tangle.

Grunting and straining, Gulliver had almost climbed atop the farmer when a deep voice shouted, *"Gulliver!* What are you doing?"

The young soldier was distracted for a split second. That was all the farmer needed. He pulled his knees close to his chest and shoved his feet against Gulliver's breastplate with all his might. Gulliver flew sprawling into a mud puddle two yards away as the farmer leaped to his feet and dashed off.

Gulliver jumped up and shook a fist after the fleeing peasant. "You'll be sorry!" he raged. "I hope you enjoy your fate, you—" Suddenly, he realized who had called his name. He froze with his fist still in the air.

Slowly, he turned his head. Sure enough. Leading a ragtag band of 35 or 40 peasants into the city, the Captain of the Guard, mounted upon his noble steed, paused long enough to stare down at Gulliver.

Embarrassed, Gulliver tried to brush the soil from his jersey. "I . . . I was rescuing him, Your Honor. Compelling him to come in, if you please. I . . . I . . . " He knelt suddenly, and only too late realized his sword hung between his legs. His chin bounced off the hilt.

"What were your orders, soldier?" the Captain demanded.

Head bowed, Gulliver spoke so quietly that the wind nearly covered his voice. "Ride forth and warn, sir. If necessary, escort."

"Gulliver," the Captain said gently.

He had never called Gulliver in that tone before. The young soldier dared to lift his head.

Mounted on his steed, clouds swirling behind him, the Captain looked as if he might command the very storm itself. In his steely eyes, though—compassion. "No one has ever been argued into the King's City. And if they were, they would not stay. The King can only rule and protect those who want Him."

"I was only trying—"

"I know. But while you wasted yourself upon that peasant, you could have warned a dozen others who, once told, would have rejoiced to make their way through the One Gate." Seeing Gulliver's downcast expression, the Captain added, "The King and I only hold you responsible for what part *you* can do, not what the hearers do. Let that thought guide you."

Lightning and thunder pealed once, twice, and yet again. A steady but light rain began to fall, precursor of the fury yet to come. The Captain gathered his reins in one gauntlet and prepared to ride. "The time is yet short. Now *go!*"

Gulliver scrambled to obey. He leaped onto his horse. As it pranced backward, he saluted the Captain.

The Captain flashed a grin. "I see your heart, soldier, and

your failure is reckoned unto you as victory. The only time you must truly succeed is the last time you try."

Another burst of lightning struck, blinding Gulliver. When he blinked his eyes back into focus, the Captain was gone.

Dazed, Gulliver paused, staring at the citadel's stone wall yet not seeing the rain glide down it. Conflicting emotions ran through him. He was an idiot! There was no end to the depth of his foolishness! Yet, the Captain had *smiled* upon him!

What was it he had said? "The only time you must truly succeed is the last time you try."

As the sky grew darker, a smile grew on Gulliver's face. With a shout of command he wheeled the horse about and galloped toward his second chance.

The Sword of Joy

WHEN THE King's outpost was still two leagues away, Sasha finally heard the beast pursuing her. She looked behind her, but night draped like funeral clothes over the forested road, hiding the monster.

The creature had seduced her parents, perhaps even killed them, but she would not let it take her. Fear overcame her weariness and pushed her to a trot. If the stories were true, the outpost held her only hope of escape.

The crackling and thrashing of its passage through the forest behind her drew nearer. Despite the chill night wind that sliced through her pauper's garb, Sasha's perspiration began to plaster her black bangs to her forehead. Now she ran.

The loping beast surprised a nest of wild pheasants sleeping in the bush. They burst into the moonlight with loud, sudden squawks, startling Sasha. She screamed. She ran faster. Her throat burned from gulping air.

The girl pounded barefoot around a bend in the road, and the lights of the King's outpost came into view. A desperate sob escaped her as she saw how far it was.

Behind her, the beast drew ever closer. Besides the snapping of leaves and branches, she could now hear the creature's fiendish snarling.

She didn't know if the beast could talk, but it could force mental impressions upon humans. That was part of its stealthy danger. Unaided, no one could think straight when the beast thrust its hideous presence into them. She knew that something deep inside her wanted what the beast offered. If the beast succeeded in linking with that hidden part of her, she would never have a thought of her own again.

The unclean presence of the beast oozed against Sasha's mind. Shouting a furious *"No!"* as she fled, she pushed the beast out of her thoughts.

The shadowed outpost danced and blurred in Sasha's vision. Was it getting closer or farther away? Tears of panic clouded her eyes, and her head was light from exhaustion. But somehow, an indefinite time later, she found herself pounding frantically, endlessly upon the oaken gate of the outpost and shrieking for help.

A savage snarl ripped the night, close to Sasha. She whirled. Barely visible in the gloom, the beast slowed, stopped, and fixed its hypnotic eyes upon her. She had an impression of something both hairy and scaly; wolfen, yet armored like a roach. Revulsion coursed through her. She shrank back against the gate, hoping her cries had alerted someone.

Then the unholy presence touched her mind again. She

resisted. She still resisted. But gradually, she wondered why. Perhaps the creature was not so bad. Slowly, despite herself, she began to unclench her fists. Why, look, it was offering her a crystal goblet full of a beautiful sparkling lavender liquid. It was a cup full of excitement and acceptance. Her hand was reaching out for it. The beast stepped close enough to touch her . . .

The gate flew inward so suddenly that Sasha fell to the ground. The beast screamed its frustration and lashed out at her with ten-inch razor-sharp claws. She saw a sword like silver lightning meet the claws and throw them back.

The armored warrior holding the sword leaped over her and stood in the gateway between Sasha and the beast. In a low, intense voice, the guard ordered, "In the name of the King, begone!"

The beast shrieked defiance and spit a stream of acid at the guard. It splashed off the knight's armor harmlessly, but when it hit the ground sizzled and steamed. Sasha, unable to take her eyes off the confrontation, unable to find her feet, started scooting backwards through the gate.

The knight leveled the sword at the beast. "You have no place here. The King rebukes you. Now go!" The point of the sword rushed at the beast's chest as the guard lunged, but the beast was quicker. Snarling and yelping, it fled into the darkness.

The guard slammed the gate shut and barred it, then knelt before Sasha, who was gasping and trembling. "It cannot come in here. You are safe now."

"Protect me!" Sasha pleaded. "Not tonight only, but until the beast no longer pursues me!"

"Protection can be arranged. But do you know the terms? You must serve the King with all your heart for all your life, and Him only shall you serve!"

Sasha sat in the dust of a parade ground, which now began spinning around her head. "I will! I pledge!" she panted. The last thing she saw was the knight's helmet being removed, and the look of concern on the knight's face. The last thing she felt was surprise that the warrior was a woman, old enough to be her mother.

Then Sasha fainted away.

▣ ✠ ▣

Morning light bathed the room when Sasha's eyes blinked open. The sunlight streaming through the ivy-bordered window warmed the stone walls. She found herself in a real bed, softer than the pile of straw she slept on at home. A crude wooden table, two chairs, and a basin of water furnished the room.

She sat up and only then realized that someone had dressed her in a soft white nightgown. Her old clothes were gone. And she noticed one other thing, a painful throbbing in her shoulder. She pulled the neck of the nightgown to one side and found four short, parallel slashes where the beast had struck at her.

Last night's terror was all too vivid in her mind. She shuddered. The beast had nearly won, just like it had with her parents. They now drank the beast's potions every day, still believing they were not under its spell. Their cottage had fallen into disrepair and their crops kept shrinking while Sasha's parents spent most of their time surly and intoxicated. The beast had convinced them that their experiences with the arcane potions made them better than their sober acquaintances—of which there were few left. The beast's power permeated Sasha's entire village.

She had tried the potions twice. They tasted wondrous and at first brought joy to the heart. Had she not awakened the next day horribly sick, she could not have begun to guess that the drinks disguised slow death.

When the beast had first appeared to her, it was small and charming. It entertained her. But the beast had many different guises. The more she distrusted and tried to oppose it, the more of its strength and wildness she discovered.

Just then, the door to her room opened quietly. The smiling lady knight who had saved her last night entered, bringing cream and steaming porridge on a tray. She wore a uniform colored deep red. Her hair was changing from blonde to silver, and ended bluntly near her jaw line. "So! You are awake. How are you?"

Sasha felt shy. The woman had an air of authority. "Fine, thanks to you, milady—?" She paused, having no idea how to properly address the woman.

"I am known by many names, but my friends simply call me Faith." The lady guard sat gracefully on the edge of Sasha's bed and handed her the tray. The porridge smelled heavenly. Gently, she asked, "Do you remember your pledge from last night?"

"Yes, Milady Faith. I have little to offer the King, but I am glad to serve. Mayhap you need a scullery maid. I can cook some, and sew more. Or . . ."

Faith chuckled softly. "You know little of the King's army, I see. You will do none of those things."

"I know nothing else, milady. What else will I be?"

"What is your name, young one?"

"Sasha."

"Mm. 'Tis a fighting name, bestowed by a rebellious people. It is no longer who you are."

Faith stood and drew her sword. It fairly leapt from the hilt. As Faith held it upright, it gathered the sunlight and then reflected it back into the room in golden spangles. The blade, keen and straight, bore intricate inscriptions over its entire length, some in red. Even Sasha could tell that this was a sword to be reckoned with.

Suddenly the blade swung toward Sasha, who flinched. But Faith merely rested it on her shoulder. Suddenly using the same commanding voice she had used on the beast, Faith said, "You have had a name of war, yet lived in fear. Now you shall have a name of meekness, yet be a warrior indeed." The blade switched to the other shoulder. "You are Sasha no more. Henceforth, you are Charity Joy."

The sword sang its way back into the sheath. Faith unbuckled it and dropped it on the bed. "This blade is now yours. Each person who serves the King has one. It is best used with great cheer."

But the speechless young girl had found her tongue. "A *warrior?* Nay, Faith, I have neither strength nor skill—nor even desire! What kind of army lets maidens—"

"There is no time for such talk. As soon as you have broken your fast and dressed, meet me downstairs."

Dozens of questions and denials crowded Charity Joy's mind, but as Faith put her hand on the doorknob to leave, Joy could only blurt out, "What for?"

"For sword drill, of course." The slam of the closing door cut off all possibility of protest.

▦ ✝ ▦

"Now, Joy," the guard told her, "Draw your sword and begin to learn."

For a moment Sasha stood stupidly, wondering who Joy was. Then she remembered that it was she; Faith had changed her name.

"This is not right," Sasha insisted. "You tricked me into this."

"Draw your sword," Faith said.

With an awkward, jerky motion, Sasha managed to drag the long sword from the scabbard fixed around her waist. She was not prepared for its weight, and the point immediately dropped to the dust.

She flushed with embarrassment and glanced around the courtyard to see if anyone had witnessed her. Within the stone arches of the fort, other new recruits trained, too. Each had his own tutor. A class of intermediate soldiers took turns charging a jousting dummy. Veteran soldiers went about routine duties. Servants drew water from the well. Everyone seemed too busy to notice her.

Suddenly the point floated in the air, lifted by the tip of her teacher's sword. "It is too heavy to use in your own strength," Faith said. The knight had changed from her ruby uniform to loose-fitting pants and shirt. Of indeterminate age, she looked slender yet muscular and carried an indefinable air of bravery. "But if you learn to balance it, you and the sword work together. Try pointing it upward."

Sasha needed both hands to bring the sword erect. But once she got the tip high enough to point at her teacher's chin, the sword seemed to settle back into her hand comfortably. It felt taut and ready, almost living. "But I . . ."

"It takes very little to defend yourself," Faith continued. "If a weapon comes toward your chest, simply move your sword hand a few inches from right to left. The sword pushes the weapon to the side so that it cannot hit you. Try it." In slow motion, she thrust her own sword at Joy.

Startled at facing any sword, no matter how slow, Sasha completely failed to respond. She gaped at the oncoming blade until Faith stopped.

"No, Joy. A simple move, right to left along your waist. Like this." Faith demonstrated in a short, efficient gesture. "Lift the blade and try again."

"But this is a mistake!" Sasha protested, now with more fire. "War is for brave men, not delicate handmaidens!"

Faith settled herself into a combat position. "It must be this way. Friends of the King have many enemies. Lift the blade."

Instead, Sasha firmly sheathed her blade. "I will gladly serve if you give me some other task. I'll wash dishes. I'll even play chimney sweep! But I cannot do this—*awp!*"

Faith's blade darted in and pricked Sasha in four separate spots before Sasha could defend herself.

"Very good," Faith said coolly. "Simple motion, right to left—now!" She lunged.

Flinching, Sasha parried. The swords clashed. Faith held still with her sword point piercing the air to Sasha's side, so that the girl could see how well the defensive move worked.

"Well done." Faith resumed the attack stance. "We'll do it again."

"No, I don't want to!"

"You must."

"Why?"

"Because it must be."

"That is no answer!" Sasha stared at Faith, filled with anger. She could hardly imagine a more unreasonable person. "You are no teacher at all."

"I am your only teacher. Without me, you cannot please the High King."

Defiance welled up in Sasha. "And if I refuse to obey you?"

Faith gazed back as if from a great height, suddenly remote. "If you disobey me, you cannot stay."

"So say you, but you do not mean it. The woman who saved my life would not return me to the beast."

"I would not be doing so. You would."

The young woman and the old woman matched cold stares for long moments.

"Lift your blade, Charity Joy," Faith commanded.

"Call me by my real name! I am Sasha, and I will not fight because I cannot! If you send me to war, I will die!"

"All who will not learn from me also die," Faith answered. With hardly a pause, she added, "You are free to go." She turned her back and walked away.

"Faith!" Sasha shouted. But the guard kept crossing the courtyard, as though the girl did not exist.

Sasha swallowed hard. Her choice was no choice at all. Die tonight outside the walls, or die later as an unskilled fighter.

"Faith!" But the woman warrior seemed deaf. Her back grew smaller as she strode away.

Sasha fought back tears of frustration. The wound in her shoulder, where the beast had left its claw marks, began to burn as if coming alive.

She lifted her sword and ran after Faith.

◈ ✝ ◈

For a week, Sasha reported to the courtyard early each morning and spent most of the day being Faith's pupil. Although she complained less, she still hated the workouts. She began to regret ever pledging to serve the King.

She did not make friends with anyone. She met new recruits, but most spoke a foreign language. Many seemed so happy and well-adjusted that she distrusted them instantly. At mealtimes, she ate alone. Even as miserable as life had been back in her village, she became homesick for it.

By the end of the week, the reluctant student had learned two parries well enough to perform them at combat speed. But her muscles were sore and she could not perform any thrust well enough to prevent an enemy from slicing her arm off when she extended it.

Daily, she argued with Faith. Sasha resented the way Faith explained almost nothing. The guard told Sasha what to do, then remained silent when the girl demanded to know why. Twice when Faith refused to answer Sasha's questions, the girl threw her weapon in the dust and stormed off to her room to sulk. On both occasions, she awoke the next morning to find her sword cleaned and waiting on her table.

By the end of two weeks, she had lost weight and the soreness had passed from her muscles. She could practice longer without losing her breath. The sword did not feel quite as foreign, but so what? She did not intend to use it in real combat.

The nights were the worst. Separated from her old friends and having no new ones, she could do nothing but stare out her third-floor window until bedtime.

And on many nights, she saw the beast. Whenever she did, the old wound in her shoulder would begin to burn.

The creature would slink from the forest to prowl about

the walls of the outpost, in dim moonlight slavering and testing the walls. She wondered what its intentions were until one night it turned, raised its head, and stared directly at her. She ducked out of sight, but their eyes had met briefly. She knew then with chilling certainty that it still hungered for her. It was searching for a way in.

▣ ✝ ▣

The scabbard on her hip slapped at her legs over and over as she fled up the winding stone stairs. She blinked back tears of fury. This had been the worst fight with Faith yet.

Faith had commanded her to join the midnight patrol outside the walls tonight. She had reacted so strongly at the order that this time Faith was chasing her.

She reached the corridor and dashed for her room. She made it to the oaken door, slammed and barred it, and backed away, still breathing hard.

It was only then that she heard the low growl behind her. Suddenly her nearly-healed shoulder wound seemed to catch fire.

Sasha whirled. She screamed.

The beast had never looked the same way twice. This time it was all fangs and claws, with a mouth inside its mouth and several arms. It was nearly twice as tall as Sasha. It dragged its last leg in through the window and circled warily toward the girl. Its foul presence nearly overpowered her on the spot, but she managed to edge away from it, staying on the opposite side of the small chamber.

The doorknob rattled. The door shook with blows, but the bar held firm. The creature grinned two grins, moving between Sasha and the door.

At last Sasha understood. Faith had kept the beast out. Locking Faith out had let the beast in.

Tears of terror streamed down Sasha's face as she freed her sword from its scabbard. The tip of the sword fell to the ground just as it had the first time she used it. Struggling not to gag at the foul stench that thickened the air, she raised the point.

Beast and girl circled. For a moment her eyes locked with it, and it battered a thought into her mind:

Surrender now and I might not kill you

A sob escaped Sasha's throat. She shook her head once, as much to shake tears from her eyes as to say no, and clenched the sword handle with both fists. She could only wait; she did not know how to attack.

The creature grinned at her sword. From behind its back, it produced a sword of its own, blade black and shiny as midnight. Sasha gasped.

The pounding grew fiercer at the chamber door.

From behind its back the beast drew another sword, and another, and another. It stepped toward Sasha and screamed a scream of evil joy.

The malicious presence pressed on her as though she lay many fathoms under the sea. It smashed at her with waves of blind, unreasoning despair: *useless to resist*cannot win *all alone*my strength far beyond yours*never stop chasing

64 SCOTT & RENEE PINZON

you cannot win—

Sasha's voice was low, and it trembled, but the resolve
in it stopped the beast. "Nay," she breathed. Some of her
poorly-practiced training was returning to her. "Nay!" At last
she remembered to balance the sword, and it became part
of her. Its strength seemed to flow into her. "Greater is He
that is in me!"

The beast shrieked and hurled itself at her. Flinching, she
closed her eyes and let the sword have its way.

The momentum of the creature's onslaught hurled her
back against the wall, knocking the wind out of her. The im-
pact bulged her eyes open. She saw four swords poised to
butcher her. And her sword in the beast's chest.

Now it was the creature's eyes that showed terror. It fell
backwards, then slithered for the window. It plunged into
the twilight, leaving Sasha's sword and a trail of slime behind.

The pounding on the oaken door reached a crescendo
as the support holding the bar across the door gave. The
door flew open and a woman warrior, followed by several
soldiers, burst into the room.

Sobbing, Sasha threw herself into the arms of Faith.

☖ ✝ ☖

The indignant young woman dashed her sword to the
dust and shouted, "I refuse! I am a seamstress and no fighter!"
She tried to rush from the training ground.

"Hold!" The voice crackled with command, and the
young woman froze in her tracks, back still turned. "You may

not want to visit the front lines. But if you truly serve the King, the front lines will visit you."

The teacher approached the rebellious young woman and hugged her. The girl's defiant posture wilted. "Hear this," the teacher said gently. "Run as you might, you *will* face the enemy. You might as well have a sword when you do."

At last the girl turned and nodded. She mumbled, "What would you have me do?"

"Pick up your sword," the teacher said. "The only way it will fail you is if you fail to use it. I swear it, as sure as my name is Charity Joy."

Reluctantly, the pupil took up the blade.

Charity Joy smiled warmly at her. "For that reason," she added, "it is best used with good cheer."

6

Squire of the Embers

ITH THE sun dropping behind towering pines, Gulliver Lamm, newly-appointed Squire and Knight-to-Be, picked his way among soldiers, horses, and campfires. What had been a peaceful meadow in the woods an hour ago was now jammed with colorful pavilions, armorers, wagons, and everything else needed to support a thousand knights on a long crusade when they camped for the night.

Gulliver didn't notice the aroma of the stewpots, the clusters of soldiers singing, nor even the pain in his own tired feet. This was his first campaign, and the Captain of the Guard had just sent for him. He trembled at facing the High King's own son, despite the fact that they had met before. What could the Captain possibly want with an inexperienced squire?

At the center of the camp, a purple pavilion displayed a shield near its entrance. The shield, blazing in the glow of the setting sun, bore three golden lions rampant upon a blue field of twelve six-pointed stars. Gulliver gulped, and adjusted his chain mail shirt to ride more squarely on his shoulders. He straightened his leather helm. Then he strode up to one of the guards flanking the entrance and announced his name. The guard nodded and beckoned Gulliver inside.

The guard escorted him to one of the pavilion's inner chambers, and left. Gulliver's eyes immediately went to the large, deep-chested man who was seated on a wooden chair huge and ornate enough to be a throne. The Captain's royal presence fairly made his silver breastplate glow from within. Streaks of white ran through the man's beard and flowing black hair. His blue eyes seemed to look right inside of Gulliver.

"Sire," Gulliver said, dropping to one knee and bowing his head.

In a deep voice, the Captain commanded, "Rise, Squire Lamm. You are well come."

Gulliver stood tongue-tied, trying to hide his nervousness. He turned to the other two men in the room, new squires like Gulliver, and his heart sank. There stood Bodo, a tall, skinny squire who had buck teeth, a scrawny neck decorated with a monstrous Adam's apple, and an oversized leather helm that almost covered his eyes. And there was short, fat Roland, who smelled as if he had yet to bathe this year.

He had spotted them during the first day's march because they paraded out of step, bumping into soldiers both behind and ahead of them, throwing straight rows into disarray. Stumbling, apologizing, unsure of both where they were and where they should be, the two squires made marching impossible. Gulliver wondered for the tenth time how they had made it into the King's army. All this flashed through his mind as he bowed to them formally. Being here with them must mean he was in trouble for some reason.

When Bodo bowed back, his leather helm fell off. He scrambled to pick it up, and accidentally kicked it. The helm caromed off the Captain's foot. The Captain made no comment as the mortified Bodo picked it up.

"In the week that we have been marching through the Great Forest," the Captain asked, "has anyone told you the reason for this campaign?"

The three squires looked at each other. Finally, Gulliver answered, "The King's business is his own, Sire. We are happy merely to serve."

"Well said," the Captain replied. "But now I no longer call you servants, because a servant does not know his master's business. I call you my friends. You will know the reason we march."

Gulliver nearly gasped at the honor.

"Some leagues north of here," the Captain explained, "one of our outposts is defending the border against a vast enemy army. Even now, outnumbered defenders are dying, that the kingdom might stay free."

"We must help them!" Roland cried, then clapped his hand over his mouth. It was not advisable to interrupt the Captain.

"Indeed, we shall," the Captain said. "That is why I have

mobilized such a large army. However, it will take two weeks to march this many fighters to the border. Before then, the defenders may lose hope and surrender."

The Captain stood, and spread a parchment map of Evermore on an oak table. "The army must hold to the road, else it cannot defend itself against surprise attacks. We are here. The outpost is here, due north. See how the road between them curves like the letter S?"

The three nodded. Bodo's helm slid down over his eyes. He pushed it back up.

"But a squad of soldiers could travel in a straight line from here to the outpost and reach it in a week—perhaps less." The Captain looked each man in the eye, waiting for the idea to sink in. "I think the remnant of fighters could hold out if they knew that help was on the way."

Catching on, Gulliver asked, "You are sending us to the outpost?"

The Captain said, "If there are any volunteers."

"Here am I!" Gulliver said. "Send me!" Roland and Bodo chimed in just as eagerly.

The Captain smiled at their enthusiasm, then grew serious. "It is not an easy journey. That is why I send three instead of one. One could move faster, but may lose heart. The woods are gloomy, and full of ogres. You will be separated from the rest of the army. Do you still dare to make this journey?"

"Yes!" the three said as one.

"So it is decided," the Captain declared. He produced

three written messages, each folded and sealed, and gave one to each man. "Put this message near your heart, and guard it well. It brings hope to those who fight long. Remember that in the woods, your sword can guide you as well as defend you."

The Captain gazed upon each of them. Inexplicably, when he looked upon Gulliver, his eyes seemed to sadden momentarily.

"Your cause is urgent, so you leave this evening," the Captain concluded. "Take my blessing."

◈ ✝ ◈

They hiked briskly for two hours before it grew too dark to continue safely. During that time, distractible Roland had walked into trees twice, and tripped over his own sword thrice.

As they gathered dry branches for a fire, Gulliver asked, "What do you suppose this is all about?"

Roland, bare belly hanging out from under his mail vest, looked confused. "Are we not delivering a message to the outpost?"

"We are," Gulliver agreed. "But why did the Captain entrust it to three of his most inexperienced soldiers when he had a thousand better right outside his tent?"

Bodo and Roland exchanged dull, cow-like stares. "I don't know," Bodo said, dropping an armload of firewood. It landed on Roland's foot.

Gulliver waited impatiently for chubby Roland to stop

hollering and hopping, and for Bodo to stop apologizing. When they did, he continued, "I can think of only two possibilities. First, the Captain might have a secret battle coming up that will require all his experienced men."

Roland ignited the kindling with his flint and steel, then asked, "And the other possibility?"

"I think this is a test," Gulliver replied. "The message itself might not be as important as seeing whether we can really deliver it. Perhaps that's how the Captain will decide which knight each of us serves."

Firelight flickered off Bodo's surprised expression. "I never thought of that!"

A breeze carried Roland's odor to Gulliver, who wrinkled his nose, then pressed on. "Either way, the message is very important. We must not fail."

Near the fire, Bodo had spread out the blanket he planned to sleep on. "Oh, absolutele *YIII!*" The panicking squire leaped off his sleeping roll as it burst into flames. "Roland! Gulliver! Do something!"

With disgust, Gulliver grabbed the pot of water they had intended to boil for stew, and dumped it on the blanket. Hissing and steaming, the fire went out.

"Oh, good thinking!" Bodo exclaimed. "Wasn't it, Roland?"

"Right brilliant," Roland admired.

Gulliver forced a smile. "How about if I take the first watch?" he offered.

When certain that they slept, Gulliver rolled up his pack and stole away into the forest.

◈ ✛ ◈

A pinpoint of sunlight flashed against Gulliver's chain mail, and reflected into his eyes. He woke with a start. He found himself sitting against a tree trunk. Then he remembered hiking north until the eastern sky had turned gray. He had intended to rest for just a minute. Instead, he had dozed for probably two hours.

He shook his head furiously, trying to wake himself. He rose stiffly, gauged the angle of the sun, and found north. Then he resumed walking.

Except for the sunbeam that woke Gulliver, shadows ruled the thick forest. Pines and larch towered overhead, branches intertwining and shading the ground. Squirrels chittered and birds fluttered, but the trees muffled the sounds. The gloom seemed almost sinister.

He felt badly about abandoning Bodo and Roland, but two things the Captain had said motivated him. The cause was urgent and one could move faster than three. He only hoped they could find their way back to the main host without setting themselves on fire or knocking themselves out on trees.

The day passed without incident. He rested seldom and briefly, pushing further and further north. The next day was the same. Despite the fact that he had marched three solid days on only six hours' sleep, he was making rapid progress toward the outpost. All in all, things went well—thus far.

◈ ✛ ◈

On his third night in the woods, ogres filled his dreams, vicious ogres with claws and fangs. Forest ogres with mean tiny eyes and oversized heads and matted fur. Great gray ogres that loved human flesh above all foods and could rip a man's limbs off as easily as men break a wishbone.

Something hit Gulliver on the forehead, and he woke with a startled cry. Wild-eyed, he looked up. It was raining. Drops could not penetrate the tangled trees, but they gathered on branches until they became too fat for the leaves to hold. As he watched, he saw three huge drops plummet forty feet to splat upon his head. That was what had awakened him.

Gradually his speeding heart slowed to a normal pace. Still, he felt frightened. His utter aloneness became real to him for one moment. This spot seemed tainted; a scene of fear and dark dreams. He snatched his pack and fled.

For most of the morning he skirted a large bog. Low mists hid his path, and the ground made sucking noises each time the squire lifted his foot. He passed the time by imagining how proud the Captain would be at how fast Gulliver got the message through.

After noon, he needed to check his direction. He reached the top of a hill and looked around. Tall trees hid most of the sky. When he finally found a break in the branches and could see the sky, rain clouds concealed the sun, so he couldn't find north. But the Captain had said their swords could guide them in the woods.

Only when Gulliver reached for his sword did he realize he had left it where he slept.

The discovery stunned him. Even Bodo wasn't that stupid. He must return for it. But he did not want to lose half a day—no, an entire day, by the time he retrieved the sword and came back. As he stared at the trees, debating within himself, each tree began to look more and more like its neighbor. At last he realized that with no sword to guide him, and the sun hidden by clouds, he would never find the spot where he slept. But perhaps he could push on without the sword. Maybe he was more than halfway to the outpost anyway.

The squire spent the rest of the day wandering, unsure whether he was heading in the right or wrong direction. Many times paths that clearly seemed the right direction ended in impassable dead tangles of weed and thorn.

Eventually, wearied from a steep slope he had just climbed, he tripped on a root and fell heavily to the rain-soaked ground. The slippery mud sent him plunging down the far side of the slope, rolling and tumbling through brambles until he crashed against a tree.

Gulliver lay moaning for several minutes, but his largest wound was to his pride. Wet black loam covered him head to toe, and his clothes were ripped. When he finally stood, he felt as if he could not go on. But he knew he must; he could not stay in one place forever.

Perhaps all was not lost. For all he knew, he was close to the outpost. He felt inside his jerkin for the message of hope the Captain had given him.

It was gone.

Frantically, ignoring the pain, he rummaged through the brambles up and down the hill. He retraced his path, and searched on the road, beside the road, in his pack, in the pocket of his tabard. No use. Somewhere, sometime, the message had vanished.

Without knowing how or when, Gulliver had lost the hope he was to share with the defenders.

◈ ✝ ◈

Two nights later, a very depressed squire sat under a rock outcropping, barely out of the rain, at the bottom of a steep knoll. He stared miserably into his sputtering fire. The sun had not appeared in three days and, without it, he had remained lost. Filthy, tattered, and starving, he had wandered aimlessly through the forest. He had faded to a shadow of the squire who had marched triumphantly with the mighty host.

I wanted to be the squire of the best knight in the army, Gulliver rebuked himself, so I set forth bravely on my own. Now I have ruined everything.

He shivered and sneezed. The fire seemed to answer as a moist branch popped and threw several embers to one side. One ember, glowing red and gold, gradually faded to a gray husk as Gulliver watched.

I am that ember, he thought. The fire is the King's glorious army, blazing with light and comfort. But the hottest ember from it, on its own, soon turns to ash.

A rustling in the dark woods interrupted his reverie. Startled, he held his breath. What had caused the sound?

Prolonged silence. Another rustling, from a different direction.

From a third direction, a branch snapped, as if something heavy had stepped on it. Heavy like an ogre.

Gulliver threw dirt on the fire, plunging his little camp into darkness. With no sword to draw, he could only shrink back under the outcropping and wait.

Gradually, he discerned large gray shapes moving toward him among the trees. They drew closer and closer. Now he could hear low, hungry snarls. Closer. He spotted a gleam of moonlight reflected from a beady eye and a glistening fang. He could not outrun them. He had lost his weapons. He would die here the second they spotted him.

Suddenly a battle cry shattered the moment. The back of a man plunged into Gulliver's view, a man who had jumped off the knoll above Gulliver and landed in front of him. Holding a brace of torches in each hand, the newcomer shouted a challenge at the ogres. In the torchlit drizzle, the ogres shrank back, startled.

Next to one ogre, a stout man rose from the bushes. With a mighty swing, he broke a fat branch on the head of the monster. The ogre brayed in its own tongue, a disgusting mix of snorting and gargling, and fled.

The other ogres backed up. The man with the torches bellowed defiance and charged them, waving flames toward their faces. Behind them, another branch whistled through the air and another ogre threw its arms up and collapsed.

As Gulliver watched, amazed, the beasts turned and fled, crashing into each other in their haste to get away. Within moments, the echoes of their frightened cries had faded into the night.

The squire rose shakily. In a quavering voice, he began, "I offer you heartfelt thanks—"

The torch bearer, who had been watching the ogres flee, turned and faced Gulliver. With his widespread grin lit by the torches, there stood Bodo.

As Gulliver gasped, Roland stepped up next to him, cudgel propped jauntily across one shoulder. "How?" Gulliver stammered. "You . . . but I—"

"You left so fast," Roland smiled, "we didn't get to tell you that Bodo is the best tracker in the King's army."

Bodo added, "And that Roland is as strong as two men. Otherwise, ogres would not feel those love taps. Here. This is yours." Bodo handed Gulliver his lost sword.

Dumbfounded, Gulliver stared at the two. Finally he threw an arm around each of them and wept tears of repentance. "I have been so wrong," he confessed. "I thought I was better than you. But I am nothing—a squire to the embers."

"And a friend of the Captain of the Host," said a deep voice.

Gulliver turned, and saw the Captain himself step into the firelight. Immediately the squire prostrated himself on the ground. "I do not deserve your friendship," he said to the mud.

The Captain lifted Gulliver to his feet, and held his gaze. "There lies a mystery fit for the King," he said. "No one in my army is worthy. Yet *all* are. That is why each needs all others. That is why if one is lost, I leave the rest of the army, to find him."

"But I am not worth it," Gulliver insisted.

"To me you are." Suddenly the Captain squeezed Gulliver in a hard, masculine hug. "Oh, young squire, do not strike forth on your own again." Then he held out a mud-stained, folded paper.

Gulliver recognized his lost message of hope. He returned the hug, tears streaming down his face. Then he reached out and included Bodo and Roland. Deep in the forest, dampened by rain, they embraced until Bodo's helmet fell off, and then they all laughed.

7

The Stronghold

AFTER BODO rescued Gulliver deep in the forest, Gulliver marched next to him from then on. Still, it sometimes embarrassed Squire Lamm to be seen with his fellow squire.

Bodo had no sense of rhythm, and thus could not stay in step. As the army continued its march through the forest to relieve the outnumbered defenders of the border outpost, Gulliver tried to teach his clumsy friend how to feel the cadence, but eventually had to give up. Poor Bodo was even more frustrated by his clumsiness than was Gulliver.

One morning the inept foot soldier set a personal best by marching twenty paces in a row without mishap. When he turned his head to glance proudly at Gulliver, his helmet fell off. Bodo tripped over it and fell heavily to the ground. Two of the men marching directly behind him tumbled over Bodo, and soon a sizable pileup of tangled bodies had accumulated. Eventually some of the knights further ahead had to stop the march, leave the ranks and return to straighten out the mess.

When the army resumed marching, Bodo was mortified. It seemed the entire army knew of his blunder. He had even caused some to be injured. "Gulliver," Bodo blurted as the army filed on. "Why was I made this way? The King will never have any use for me."

"The King would never have drafted you into His army if you had no use," Gulliver answered. "Besides, you saved my life."

But Bodo was not cheered. "Of what use is a clumsy warrior?"

A wry smile toyed with Gulliver's lips. "Did I ever tell you of the first mission I ever undertook for the King? Before I was a squire, before I hardly knew which end of my sword to hold."

Bodo grinned. "That is very little knowledge, indeed. Say on."

Gulliver gathered his thoughts for a few paces, then began. "I was assigned with a detail of knights to storm a rebel stronghold, capture the rebels inside, and then destroy the stronghold."

Bodo looked impressed. "That does not sound like a novice's job."

"It seemed not. This was a fearsome stronghold called Vanity, a place where many died and many others vanished never to return. Most of it lay beneath the surface of the ground."

"Why did the King send you on such a dangerous quest? You are not of fearsome stature nor unusually powerful arm."

Gulliver gave one short laugh. "Rather the opposite! I was even skinnier then than I am now—not half the weight of the other knights."

"Then why did the King—"

"Patience, good Bodo. You shall see. Now, where was I? We took the stone keep above ground with almost no resistance. Such strongholds often make a show of surrendering in hopes that the army will consider them defeated and leave them alone. But the real danger began when we found the trap door leading underground . . ."

◨ ✛ ◧

Young Gulliver was the last one down the ladder into the dark. He tried to see around the broad backs of the six knights ahead of him, but he could see only the dungeon walls that fell within the circle of his torch light. Picture-language drawings covered the walls. Some were beautiful; many were extremely vulgar.

"Who made these?" Gulliver asked Deborah, the female knight next to him.

"The people who live here—the Thots," she replied. "They are elusive, rarely captured. They can be good or bad. But evil Thots try to force their will on you so that you do their evil for them. That's why the King wants them all brought into obedience."

"Quietly now," Sir Godfrey whispered. The whisper echoed in the stone labyrinth. Somewhere nearby, liquid dripped into a puddle and echoed back. "We want to surprise them. Stay together. This place is built on treachery."

Gulliver trembled from fear, excitement, and the subterranean chill. He clenched his sword in one hand and a torch
in the other. He followed the larger soldiers into a lofty room
where arched passageways opened in every direction, each
leading to darkness.

Despite the danger, this dungeon-like maze fascinated
Gulliver. As the cluster of knights slowly turned, surveying
each direction, Gulliver wandered absently toward an arch-
way. Suddenly, a mischievous draft snuffed out his torch.

Gulliver was plunged into darkness. Startled, he spun
and looked back at his torchlit troop.

"This is the largest stronghold I've seen," Sir Godfrey was
saying. "The Thots must have been adding to it for years—
where's Gulliver?"

"Here," Gulliver said. He spoke louder than he had intended; his own voice startled himself and echoed repeatedly in the room. More quietly, he added, "My torch blew
out."

"I warned you to stay with the group," Sir Godfrey said
sternly. "Now very carefully, walk toward me."

Gulliver ambled toward his troop leader. The young foot
soldier was almost to the group when he heard a soft click
under his forward foot. If he had been armored and walking rapidly, he wouldn't have heard it. He stopped in his
tracks and peered at the floor. It appeared to be made of
large flagstones, but without a torch he couldn't make out
any details.

"Don't move!" Sir Godfrey urged. "You have set off a trap!" The experienced knight positioned himself four feet ahead of Gulliver and braced himself. Legs spread wide, half crouching, he ordered, "Now jump to me!"

Gulliver leaped for Sir Godfrey. The chunk of floor that had been between them fell away, revealing a deep shaft. He fell against the knight who wrapped a strong arm around the lad's waist and clung grimly. Gulliver's feet did not clear the shaft and, for one terrifying moment, he thought he would fall in. He flailed his arms, searching for balance, and his dead torch plummeted into the hole.

Then Godfrey threw himself backwards. They both collapsed to the floor and lay panting for several breaths. Seconds later, they heard the torch splash into water far below. They heard strong jaws snapping and something muscular thrashing in the water. A horrible odor rose up out of the shaft. Then, sinister and silent, the fallen flagstone swung back into place, as before.

Wide-eyed, Gulliver couldn't speak. Even some of the older knights murmured in dismay at what had nearly happened.

Sir Godfrey stood and said, "Vanity is deceitful and desperately wicked. Now you know why it must be torn down. Everyone follow me—with caution."

Godfrey led the knights into the largest of the passageways. They crept down a corridor for several minutes. Ahead, a lantern appeared around a corner, followed by a scaly face. The face looked startled and disappeared.

"Charge!" Sir Godfrey commanded. "Catch him before he can warn others!"

The knights pounded down the corridor and around the corner. A band of Thots stood listening anxiously to the one who had seen the soldiers. At the sight of the swords, the Thots scattered in all directions.

Sir Godfrey, in the lead, managed to snag a particularly filthy one and pierce it with his sword. The other knights wrestled with other Thots. Battle sounds echoed in the stone corridor. Fiery darts bounced off armor; swords rang against hardened hides.

Gulliver, frightened, forgot all his training. He squeezed his eyes shut and began flailing his sword in all directions. Then he felt the flat of it smack something, and he heard a howl. He opened his eyes.

All the Thots were gone. One of the King's knights was rubbing a sword-shaped red welt on his forearm. He glared balefully at Gulliver and barked, "Use your sword against your enemies, not your brothers! You made me lose track of my Thot!"

Gulliver hung his head in shame. Again he had hindered the war party. Why had the King sent him on a mission when he was worse than worthless?

By the time the troop reorganized, it was too late to pursue the slippery Thots. Godfrey had killed two of the worst ones outright, but many of the others had escaped. Straightening his helmet and readjusting his breastplate, Sir Godfrey said, "We'll finish exploring this passageway. Maybe we'll find another knot of them."

They followed the passageway, turning their faces from the vulgar pictograms on the walls. The corridor stopped abruptly at a dead end. Several oil lamps mounted on niches in the wall lit an ornate gold-framed mirror hanging there, amidst miniature sculpted cherubs and demons.

The knights surveyed the mirror curiously. They could see themselves, rumpled and soiled from their battle. "Mere distraction," Godfrey said. "We'll retrace our path to the main room and explore another passage."

The soldiers all left, except Gulliver and a handsome bearded knight. Gulliver was curious about the mirror and the statues on the wall around it. The knight was staring into the mirror. Gulliver could see the reflection of the man's face; the knight was pleased at what he saw. The man struck a noble pose, then broke into a grin of satisfaction. Gulliver had to admit the mirror reflected a strikingly handsome, strong soldier.

But the reflection began to change. As the knight kept staring into it, his face no longer looked so splendid. As Gulliver watched, the face changed into a bug-eyed, crater-laden mess crowned by a bulbous, wart-filled nose. The knight cried out in dread.

Frozen with horror, Gulliver stood in shock as the face changed again—back to the handsome one.

The troop had walked away without noticing that two of its members had remained. But now Deborah ran back to them, calling, "Get away from that mirror!"

Gulliver took a last yearning glance at the enchanted mirror. Longingly, he reached out and touched one of the little sculpted demons. Deborah cried out a warning, but too late.

Immediately a sparkling gold powder dropped from overhead and wafted down upon the knight entranced by the mirror. He dropped his weapons and his shield and grasped the mirror with both hands, staring deep into it in alternating horror and joy as his face changed back and forth.

"You released one of the most potent spells the Thots have," Deborah moaned to Gulliver. "Now Baldor will never leave the enchanted mirror." She tried to pull the knight away, but he stubbornly clung to the mirror and shrugged her off.

Sorrowful that he hadn't listened to Deborah's warning, Gulliver said, "We could force him—"

"He would only return the moment we let go of him. Nothing can break the spell of self-absorption except the touch of the King."

"I'll stay with him and guard him until the King comes," Gulliver pledged recklessly.

"Then two are caught in the trap instead of one. We need you. Come, rejoin the troop."

It didn't seem right. In fact, nothing about his being here seemed right. But reluctantly, Gulliver followed her.

Back in the hall of arches, Deborah told Sir Godfrey what had happened. Gulliver looked away uncomfortably as Deborah finished her story.

"Come here, young man," Sir Godfrey ordered. Gulliver, head hanging, approached the commander. "Stay by my side at all times. Perhaps if I watch over you I can save you and the rest of us from further mishap. Now—onward."

The soldiers entered another corridor. In this one, the walls were made of gigantic stone bricks, three feet by three feet. The passage wound and split and became a maze. Godfrey led on, always veering to the right at each fork. Gulliver stayed alongside, hating himself.

Marching in the lead, Sir Godfrey came around a corner and stepped on a string set three inches off the ground in the gloom. The troop froze as a groaning sound emanated from overhead. They held their torches higher, and saw cracks shoot through the ceiling even as they watched.

"A trap!" Sir Godfrey shouted. "Run!"

But the tunnel was too narrow for six people. Before they could flee, the walls and ceiling collapsed with a thunderous clatter of stone on stone. Years of dust flew into the air, and the torches went out. The stronghold turned black as coal.

When the cave-in finally stopped, Gulliver found himself flat on the floor, on his stomach, wedged between two bricks. He couldn't see any of the other soldiers—nor even his hand in front of his face—but he could hear coughing and retching. There was a moan of pain from somewhere behind him.

And then, thankfully, there was Sir Godfrey's voice. "Sound off by rank. Name and condition."

All of the troop spoke in turn. All were alive, all were injured to some degree, and most were pinned immobile under the huge granite blocks. Gulliver, having the lowest rank, answered last.

After a long pause, Godfrey's voice said in the dark, "It could have been worse. But none of us escaped the trap. Can anyone reach their flint and steel and a torch?"

After a moment a single torch flared to life. By its light, Gulliver saw a foot inches from his eyes, and a granite block against his cheek. The crude oversized blocks leaned against one another, leaving small pockets where a person could sit or lie without being crushed.

"What do we do, Sir Godfrey?" one of the soldiers cried.

"I know not. Eventually the Captain of the Guard will send someone to see why we never reported back, but we are two days' march away from the Citadel. We could be trapped here for at least four days."

A stunned silence met the news. They all knew that a soldier could not survive that long without water.

While the commander spoke, though, Gulliver wriggled and writhed and dragged himself by his elbows. Slowly, he kept working his way through gaps between the blocks. At times he had to bend into impossible angles, and once he was certain he had gotten stuck. But with grim resolve he pushed on, leaving a layer of skin behind.

"Sir Godfrey," he said finally.

Godfrey sounded annoyed. "What is it, Gulliver?"

"I am free."

✦ ✝ ✦

Bodo laughed. "So that's why the King sent such a skinny stripling along! None of the others could fit between those rocks! "

"They gave me the torch, and from there it was simple," Squire Lamm finished. "I took all left turns to get out of the maze. Once out of the stronghold, I returned with water for the troop. Then I ran for help."

"So on your first mission, you saved them all," Bodo marveled.

"Yes, but not because of skill—because of the very way I was made. The King knows who to send, and when, and why."

Bodo sighed. "But sometimes I believe my weakness is stronger than His strength."

"It is not your ability or inability that matters," Gulliver said. "Only your availability. Besides," he added, "during this entire story, you did not stumble once!"

Bodo almost fell down from sheer surprise. Gulliver's hand shot out and steadied his friend's oversized helmet. Laughing together, they marched with the rest of the army, whose commander always led them from victory to victory.

8
Wonder and the Warpen

CONTENTEDLY HIKING back from sentry duty around one of the King's borderland outposts, Squire Gulliver Lamm was not watching the forest floor until the toe of his felt boot kicked the small animal. The little woodland creature bounced across the ground a few yards, rolled to a halt, and then blinked huge sad eyes at him.

The squire dropped his pack and knelt in the leaves by the tiny creature, afraid he had injured it. He had never seen anything like it. It was reptilian but plump, like a small turtle with no shell. The shape of its head and its alert brown eyes reminded him of a squirrel—or, more accurately, a squirrel with scales. It stared back at him. It looked neither defiant nor afraid. Instead, its expression showed curiosity.

Gulliver had neither seen nor heard of such an animal. He hesitated to touch it. Instead, he tried to reassure it with his voice. "Poor small one. I mean you no harm."

"Then why did you kick me?" the creature asked in a mouse's chirp.

Gulliver gasped. For a moment he thought the creature had actually spoken.

The creature sat back on its haunches and raised its front legs off the ground as if to scrutinize Gulliver better. In words pronounced so rapidly they tumbled over one another, it repeated, "Why did you kick me if you mean me no harm?"

Gulliver's eyes searched the woods around him, trying to see what prankster was throwing his voice from behind a tree or a bush. Finally his eyes returned to the miniature wild thing. Against better judgment, he said, "It was an accident. I didn't see you."

"Who are you?" it piped.

"Gulliver Lamm."

The creature cocked its head to one side. "A lamb? You don't look like a lamb. Aren't you taller than a lamb? And less furry? Are you *certain* you're a lamb?"

The squire laughed with delight. "Call me Gulliver if you prefer. What is your name?"

Again in its high-pitched, rushed way, it said, "I have no name. I never needed one before. You can give me one if you want."

"But how is it you can speak?"

"I don't know." The creature dropped down to all fours again and, with one of its hind legs, scratched behind its ear.

"But what are you?"

"I don't know." The big watchful eyes blinked at Gulliver.

The squire let his breath out in amazement. "You are a wonder, that's for certain," he said.

"Wonder?" the creature said. "Is that my name?"

Gulliver laughed again, and picked up his pack. "It might as well be. I see you are not injured, so I must be going."

"Where?"

"To the outpost. I am a soldier for the High King."

Wonder scuttled in an excited circle around Gulliver's feet. "I have never seen the King, have you? Wouldn't you love to see the King? Can you take me with you? I would love to see the King."

Gulliver stared at Wonder in surprise. "You are willing to come with me?"

Wonder rose up on his hind legs and chirped, "Yes, please take me. I accept."

Again Gulliver laughed. He placed his pack on the ground and opened it. "Come on, then," he said.

With a squeal of delight, Wonder scampered into the pack.

✠

How foolish I was to let this drop, Gulliver thought as he closed the door gently behind him. He had just come from an audience with the Captain of the Guard, and a sense of marvelous good fortune filled him

Meeting the Captain had been scary at first. After all, the Captain was the son of the High King Himself. Before Gulliver entered the Captain's chamber, he had thought over everything he had done in the last week, hoping the Captain wouldn't scold him for some trespass. But the Captain

only wanted to encourage and instruct Gulliver so his sol-
diering would be easier and more meaningful. The squire
still glowed at the private words of praise the Captain had
just spoken to him.

Best of all, he's willing to meet with me every day!
Gulliver exulted in his mind. Why, if I receive his advice and
training each day, I'll never lose a battle. I'll—

A distraction cut Gulliver off in mid-thought. He had
descended from the Captain's chamber in the outpost tower
to the courtyard. A group of soldiers and knights had gathered, muttering and speculating, around a parchment
pinned to the oaken gates with a dagger.

Gulliver stood on tiptoe, trying to see over the broad
shoulders of the crowd. Finally a pair of men wandered
away, deep in discussion over the writing on the parchment,
and he could see it:

To All in the King's Army
Menacing creatures called Doubts
are invading the kingdom.
Beginning immediately, all soldiers must obey
the following rules regarding Doubts:

1. *Do not seek them out; they are deadly.*
2. *If you chance to encounter a Doubt, bring it
   without delay to the Captain of the Guard.*
3. *Upon bringing a Doubt to the Captain, you must
   stay and watch the Captain slay it.*

"But it doesn't tell us what they look like!" one man was exclaiming. "It isn't fair! How will we know when we see one?"

A lady soldier replied firmly, "I have heard that one Doubt does not resemble another. No edict could describe them all. We know they must look menacing."

A man-at-arms protested, "If they're so deadly, how can we bring them to the Captain? Shouldn't we just kill them ourselves?"

"That's right!" the first man said. "You could bring the carcass to the Captain!"

A blacksmith rejoined, "It says that only the Captain may slay them. He does not want the body; he wants the live Doubt."

The small crowd mumbled in disagreement and confusion. Fresh from his meeting with the Captain, Gulliver said, "This I know: if the King made these rules, they are both wise and attainable. We had best follow them."

The group grumbled. No one could truly disagree with Gulliver, but they did not want to look at the new edict in that way. It was easier to complain.

◈ ✛ ◈

Gulliver never felt better than in private moments with the Captain. The next morning's meeting, though, was an exception.

It started out wonderfully enough. The Captain had been warm and supporting, and Gulliver had confided a problem he had with a foot soldier who made fun of Gulliver's swordsmanship at every opportunity. The Captain reminded Gulliver of times when he had behaved with the same attitude—most recently, toward Bodo and Roland—and then revealed some of the pressures that were making the other soldier feel insecure. Gulliver actually felt compassion for the other fellow when the Captain was done, and the conversation wound up in laughter.

"Before you leave my chamber," the Captain finished, "is there anything else you want to tell me about?"

"No," the squire answered honestly.

The Captain of the Guard fixed Gulliver with a gaze that seemed to stare deep inside him. "Are you certain?"

At that moment, Gulliver remembered Wonder. He had not mentioned the little creature to anyone, partly because he wasn't sure animals were allowed in the rooms. The talking creature probably ought to be reported to the Captain.

But now Gulliver felt stupid. He had just told the Captain he had nothing to report. "I'm certain," he said. He tried to return the Captain's gaze, and found it difficult. He added lamely, "At least, nothing important enough to trouble you with, sir."

The Captain held his gaze a moment longer.

Gulliver thought, *He knows I'm covering up.*

The Captain smiled and said, "Very well. Go with my blessing, faithful soldier."

Gulliver didn't analyze why the blessing stung. He was simply relieved to get out of there.

⊞ ✛ ⊞

Late at night, a single candle lit Gulliver's small room. Darkness gathered in the corners where the stone walls met one another. He had barred the door so no one could interrupt him. His pack sat open on the crude wooden table, and Wonder squatted on hind legs on the tabletop, using his forepaws to hold the grapes the squire fed him.

Wonder ate the same way he did everything—quickly and nimbly. He paused before devouring the next grape. Eyes wide with curiosity, he asked, "But how do you know the side you fight on is the right side? Don't the soldiers in the other army believe in their cause just as much as you do yours?"

"I never thought about it," Gulliver said. "I reckon they must, for they are willing to die for their Pretender King."

"Die?" Wonder squeaked. "You kill them? Isn't your King loving and good?"

"He is. The rebels can choose to surrender and join our army, but many would rather die."

Wonder looked confused. "So you believe it is right for your King to kill anyone who does not follow him? What of those who have never even heard of your King?"

Gulliver's expression darkened. Wonder, through simple curiosity, had taken the squire's mind to thoughts he had never considered. Was it possible the King was being too ruthless? "Perhaps . . ." the squire began, but a sound stopped him short. The reptile squirrel must have heard it too, for he looked frightened. He spun in circles, looking for the cause of the sound.

It came again—the distant, sobbing moan of a woman in horrible trouble. Something about how the voice echoed, as if emanating from some strange otherworld, raised Gulliver's hackles. Instinctively, he felt for the hilt of his sword.

The moan came again, louder, and was joined by the groan of a man in awful agony; the kind of groan a man might give after being tortured so long he had no strength left to scream.

Fear coursed through Gulliver. He tried to push it down, but it rose into his throat. Still unable to tell where the sounds came from, his sword in the ready position, he crossed to the window and peered below, three stories to the ground. In the dark, he could see nothing but a small whirlwind spinning dead leaves in a tight upward spiral.

The voices grew louder. Now it sounded like a chorus of men and women, all driven beyond the limits of grief, shouting wordless despair and anger.

Gulliver shot a nervous glance at the door, which was still barred. The sounds came from everywhere and nowhere. Then a blast of dead leaves shot in through the window, startling a shocked cry out of the young soldier. The whirlwind blasted into the room and consumed him.

He was buried in horrifying, disembodied screams. Terrified, he fell to his knees and covered his ears. But the shrieks, as if part of the whirlwind, raced around and around him. They carried doom and pain; and worse, they carried an accusation. Panicking, he rose and flailed his sword at the wind. Heedless, the reverberating wails kept plunging around and through him, stinging him like hurricane-driven needles.

Now the horror had him screaming, too, but he couldn't hear himself. There was no way to fight this dread attack. He had to get away.

He hurled the bar from the door and plunged into the corridor. The twister and its voices stayed with him. Beyond reason, he thrashed his sword in all directions. Then he ran for his life.

He took the stairs faster than if he had fallen down them. The hellish voices bellowed louder. The wind lashed his clothes about him. Tears streaming from his face, he raced through the courtyard and fled for the outpost gates.

Suddenly one of the night watch blocked his way. "Halt!" the armored guard commanded. Gulliver barely heard through the moans and screams. He reached for the huge oaken handle, and the knight shoved him back. "The outpost is locked for the night!" the knight stated. "No one can leave."

Frantic, Gulliver slashed at the guard. The guard's sword met the attack. In three rapid blows and a twist of the wrist, the knight disarmed the squire, sending Gulliver's sword spinning through the air.

Through the bedlam of voices, Gulliver heard the guard asking incredulously, "What's wrong with you? Why would you fight me?"

Then, as suddenly as it had begun, the attack ended. The whirlwind spun across the courtyard, visible as a funnel of dust in the moonlight. The voices went with it. When it reached the opposite wall, it simply died away.

Gulliver collapsed to his knees, sobbing. The silence was deafening.

The knight removed her helmet and knelt at his side. "Are you well?"

He stared at her dully. She had flowing black hair and warm brown eyes, which now looked both compassionate and inquisitive. He said, "Did you not hear it?"

"Hear what?"

He gave a short, ironic laugh. "Then I must be going mad."

"I saw something," she offered. "Swirling, shapeless . . . wind."

"But you did not hear the screams?"

"No." Then understanding lit her expression. "Then it is not only legend!" she exclaimed.

He stood shakily. "What?"

"They are called Warpen," she said, sheathing her sword. "Wraiths that supposedly dwell here in the borderlands. No one knows from whence they come, nor why, but they always fill their victims with blind terror."

"Aye," he said. "They made me . . . hate myself. Without knowing why." He passed a hand across his brow, as if struggling against a spell.

"Let me help you back to your room," the guard said. She called to a second knight, "Ward the gate. I will return." The knight nodded.

Gulliver's strength returned rapidly as they crossed the courtyard. "Thank you for stopping me in my confusion. I am sorry I struck you; I knew not what I was doing."

"You did not hurt me," the knight said. "My name is Charity Joy. And yours?"

The squire stopped in astonishment. "*You* are Charity Joy? Now I know why you disarmed me so rapidly! Your swordsmanship is famous!" He grimaced. "I attacked you to my shame."

Charity Joy smiled. "The sword deserves more credit than I do; it fairly wields itself. And how can you be shamed, since I don't know who you are?"

They began walking again and started up the stairs. "I am but a squire, Gulliver Lamm by name."

Charity laughed. "Suddenly the King's army seems quite small. I have heard of you, too."

"How can that be?"

"Your rise through the ranks is faster than most. I have heard that you saved a full squad of knights on your very first mission."

"Well, yes, but . . ."

"And that you saved drowning children while stronger, more experienced men stood by, arguing about who should get the glory for saving them."

"It is true. But how—"

"Your reputation precedes you, squire. And now what knight do you serve?"

"That is to be decided still."

They had come to Gulliver's room. The door hung wide open. Dead black leaves covered the floor. Inside, the bed, chair, and washbasin had been scattered. The overturned table showed a deep gash from Gulliver's wild swordplay.

The sight of the table filled Gulliver with alarm. "Wonder!" he cried, and dived into the mess. After a moment of frantic digging, he found his pack. He rummaged inside. When he withdrew his hand, upon it sat Wonder—alive and well.

"What was that?" Wonder squeaked.

Before Gulliver could answer, an exact duplicate of Wonder scrambled out of the pack onto Gulliver's palm. The twin said, "Doesn't the King know about the screams? Why doesn't he stop them?"

Gulliver gaped in amazement. "Where did *you* come from?" he asked the twin.

"I don't know," the twin chirped.

"I don't know either," Wonder added happily.

Charity was enchanted. "They *talk!* What are they?"

"That is a good question," Gulliver said.

"Question?" the twin said. "Is that my name?"

Charity pulled off one mailed glove and reached out to pet Question.

With each stroke, it pressed its head contentedly against her hand. "Who are you?" it asked. "Why are you shiny when your friend is not?"

Gulliver and Charity laughed. "She's wearing armor," Gulliver explained.

"This creature is charming!" Charity exclaimed. "Does it have a name?"

"It might as well be Question," the squire said. "And she's yours if you want her."

"Really?" Charity asked delightedly.

"Yes. Upon one condition."

"Name it."

"Please," Gulliver said humbly, "pledge that you will not tell anyone how I acted tonight."

Charity hesitated. "Not even the Captain?"

"*Especially* not the Captain. He would never trust me again."

"I think he will. He understands much—"

"Please, swear it. As a favor to me."

Charity paused. Finally, she raised her sword, and said, "I so pledge."

Gulliver looked relieved. He took Charity's helmet from her, and placed Question in it. "Perhaps these little creatures should be our secret, too," he observed. "Why provoke needless controversy?"

"Perhaps that is wise. Some soldiers would not care, but some would be jealous, some alarmed. For the sake of unity, we will keep the secret."

Gulliver, distracted, surveyed the windblasted room, puz-zling over the attack. "Yes," he said absently. "For unity."

▨ ✛ ▨

The Warpen attacked a week later, late at night.

Gulliver was feeding Wonder, who had now grown to the size of a cat, when he heard the first faint sob. A shiver ran through his body.

He rushed to the window and shuttered it. He leaped to the door, which was already shut, and barred it. In the brief seconds that took, the sound had risen to a ghostly symphony of agony. The supernatural, unreasoning terror it brought with it began to irresistibly fill Gulliver.

"Wonder," Gulliver gulped, "you'd better hide. Hide Curiosity and Inquiry, too." The three creatures scuttled into the pack and pulled it shut behind them.

The soldier tried to steel himself, but fright turned his insides to water. An open book on the table riffled its pages in a draft. A cloud of dust and leaves slid in under the barred door, and suddenly the air in the room was alive.

The voices howled at him, lashing his hair and clothes around. The small hurricane shoved him around the room. An invisible fist seemed to squeeze his heart, and he cried out in pain. Clutching his ears, he stumbled into the table and knocked over his bed. He did not draw his sword, knowing it was useless against the roars and wailing. Instead, he grimly endured the attack. Though filled with sudden and irresistible dread, he was more afraid of bolting into the courtyard and making a fool of himself again.

The assault lasted several minutes. Then, as mysteriously

as before, it suddenly ended. One moment Gulliver could not hear his own screams; the next, he was shouting at silent stone walls.

He righted his bed and collapsed onto it. He was uninjured, but shaken. Why were these strange attacks happening? He had never heard any other soldier speak of it. He dearly wanted to speak to the Captain about it, but every time he thought of doing so, he felt the Captain would be disappointed in him for being so frightened and helpless against mere wind and voices. If he could somehow deal with the problem himself, then report it to the Captain after the problem was dispensed with, it would look better. Yes, that was how he would handle it.

Or perhaps not. Gulliver was having serious misgivings about the Captain lately. Wonder's innocent questions had caused him to rethink many things; in fact, he marveled at how little thinking he had done before Wonder. Most of the other soldiers stared uncomfortably at Gulliver when he raised the issues on his mind. Gulliver was beginning to think the others were fools. Had they never questioned whether or not there really was a High King, since no one had ever seen him? Didn't they realize that some men claimed the inscriptions on their swords were filled with errors? How could they be truly certain that the High King was the only good king? Gulliver had begun finding excuses to skip the daily meetings with the Captain, because he was no longer certain the Captain was trustworthy.

Gulliver shook his head and sat up. The only bright spot

was Charity, who understood his questions and was beginning to have a few of her own. They seemed to have more in common with each passing day. Most of all, they shared the fascinating secret of the talking animals.

Wonder and his children were crawling out of the pack. Three had gone in. Five came out.

▣ ✣ ▣

The next month brought significant changes to Gulliver. The Warpen visited him seven times in three weeks. Nothing countered their attack—not stuffing cloth under the door, not cotton plugs in his ears, not lying still and ignoring them. Nothing had worked. He had become haggard and withdrawn, and even had trouble performing daily duties such as grooming the knights' horses and polishing armor.

Tension filled his every waking moment, for it seemed he heard the Warpen whisper all day. Since the Warpen came in force when he was alone, he longed for company. But because he felt obliged to hide the most important dilemma in his life, he could not force himself to make small talk. Eventually his only company was Charity, Wonder, and more little wonders than his pack should be able to hold.

One night a loud, insistent knock at Gulliver's door startled him. He shooed his creatures into the pack and closed it, then opened the door.

Charity rushed into the room, tousled and weeping. "The Warpen," she blurted, "they just attacked me!"

"How terrible!" he exclaimed. Secretly, he was relieved

not to be the only one to suffer the attacks.

"I'm taking all my creatures to the Captain of the Guard, Gulliver."

"Why?" he demanded hotly. "That has nothing to do with the Warpen! We promised to share it as our secret!"

"Because of the King's edict," Charity responded firmly. "We don't know what the creatures are. But now I think they are Doubts."

Gulliver snorted. "Impossible. The edict says Doubts are menacing. These innocent little fellows don't even have teeth!"

"They are no longer so little," Charity pointed out. Wonder and Question had both grown to the size of bear cubs, and the other creatures followed proportionately, depending on their age. "And I question their innocence. They endlessly challenge the King."

Gulliver scooped up a couple of the newest creatures, Suspicion and Mistrust. He stroked them lovingly and replied, "They never state anything bad about the King. They simply ask questions."

"You are convinced of their innocence?"

"Confidently."

"Then why not bring them to the Captain, if you have nothing to fear?"

Gulliver blanched. "But there are so many of them now. He will be angry!"

"I am bringing him mine."

"But you *promised!*"

"First I promised to serve the King!" she shot back. Her expression softened. "I will not tell him anything about your Doubts. But I will tell him everything about mine."

"They're not Doubts! And if you go," Gulliver added, throwing his chest out and lifting his chin, "you break my trust and end our friendship."

Charity stared back at him, first with shock, then with resolve. "That is your choice," she said. "I have made mine."

▨ ✟ ▨

One minute he was asleep; the next moment, his eyes were open, alert.

Had that been the first faint sob of the Warpen?

He heard the wind pounding insistently at his shutters. Then came the echoing wails of regret and self-loathing, and the familiar terror poured through him like ice water. Any second now, it would slide in through some chink or crack and assail the room. His blood ran cold as he realized for the first time that underneath all the shrieks and bellows he could discern sinister, mocking laughter.

His barred door exploded inward with a crash and the Warpen flooded the room, twice as strong as ever before. The wind lifted him and his bed and tossed them against the farthest wall, knocking the breath out of him. Before he could clear his head, the gale-force phantom picked him up again, tossed him roughly into the middle of the room, and held him face up in midair. He kicked and struggled helplessly as the swirling Warpen yammered and howled him deaf.

Caught in the living whirlwind, the objects in the room raced in circles around his levitated body. Pots and dishes shattered against the walls; books tumbled past his head. Then his own sword floated out of the debris, unsheathed itself, and flew at him point first.

Barely in time, Gulliver slapped it aside. A thin line of blood appeared on his chest. And then, as if the tiny cut had created an entrance, the Warpen entered his heart. It felt as if they were pulling it inward upon itself, making it shrink and harden.

Animal panic renewed his struggles. With a roar, he kicked himself free of the twirling enemy and dropped to the rock-hard floor. He stood and backed up against the wall. His hand struck his pack, which somehow had remained undisturbed through all this.

One thought coursed through his mind. He had to flee, leave the outpost forever, hide someplace where the Warpen could never find him again. He grabbed the pack and fled.

On the stairs, the beast caught up with him. Gulliver kept running as the tempest tore at him with invisible claws. He was shouting back at it, gibbering without comprehension. Tears streaming from his face, he dashed through the courtyard and fled for the outpost gates.

Suddenly Charity, dressed in the armor of the night watch, blocked his way. "Halt!" she commanded. Gulliver barely heard through the moans and screams. He reached for the huge oaken handle, and she shoved him back. "You cannot leave like this!" she cried.

Gulliver had long ago quit using his sword. He raised his pack and tried to bludgeon her.

Charity dodged the blow easily and smacked the side of his head with the flat of her sword. Gulliver bellowed in fury and dismay. Caught between his personal demons and an unbeatable foe, he staggered back a step. She whacked him again, driving him back another step. Then, with powerful, stinging blows, she forced him toward the stairs.

Lost in a storm of self-hatred and dread, the squire scarcely knew where he was. All he wanted was to flee; and disallowing that, he simply wanted the Warpen to stop. But the Warpen seemed to realize where Charity herded them, and the insane screams doubled.

Then he found himself in the Captain's chambers. Despite the late hour, the Captain, in full battle gear, was ready. The Captain stood unmoving as the whirlwind tore into the room and buffeted his hair and robes.

Charity tore the pack from Gulliver and slammed it upon the Captain's oaken table. "Here are his Doubts," she cried. "Slay them!"

The Warpen screams ripped through Gulliver in a fury of rage and hatred, striking both he and Charity to the ground. The Captain said, "No."

Charity looked stunned. Lost in his torment, Gulliver could not follow what she said. The Captain replied with something about the King's edict. Finally, through the overpowering noise, Gulliver realized that the Captain had told her no one could bring another person's Doubts to the Captain. The squire cried, *"Take* them if that's what you want! If it will end this, *take them!"*

The Captain of the Guard grinned.

The Captain dumped the Doubts out of the pack onto his table. There were two dozen of them, in all sizes, and each one hit the table writhing and screaming protests until the Captain touched it. Then it would swoon and lie still.

Within seconds the Captain had all the Doubts lined up neatly on the table. He lifted his two-handed broadsword. The hurricane directed its full force at him. Furniture tumbled across the chamber, but the Captain and his table did not budge. With one blow, he beheaded every Doubt at once.

The room went instantly silent and still.

Gulliver's ears rang loudly. It took him several seconds to realize the screaming had stopped. Slowly, tentatively, he dared to remove his hands from his ears. "Is . . . is it over?" he asked.

"They are dead," the Captain assured him. He strode to Gulliver, helped the squire stand, and touched the squire's ears. The ringing stopped.

Charity struggled to her feet. The Captain draped a protecting arm around each of them, and answered their unspoken questions. "Doubts cannot hurt you unless you hide them from me," he said. "If you lack wisdom, come to me. You cannot possibly offend me with your questions, however blasphemous, if you truly desire answers."

"But," Gulliver stammered, "You did nothing to the Warpen, yet when you killed the Doubts—"

"The Doubts draw the Warpen to you," the Captain explained. "The Warpen are also known as Guilt, and the more you hide your Doubts from me, the stronger Guilt grips you. The voices of Guilt are self-accusing, wily, and suspicious, even able to turn my Father's Word against you. Guilt will poison your heart and drive you from the army unless you let me remove it from you. It is far too great a foe for you to fight yourself."

"The whole time, you knew," Gulliver realized. "You knew I was hiding this from you."

"Oh yes. But if I killed your Doubts before you were willing to bring them to me, you would simply go out and find more. Doubts would still appeal to you."

Overwhelmed, Gulliver wanted to weep, to rejoice, to laugh, to repent. Instead, he knelt, and pledged himself anew to the King's service. And then he had many, many questions to ask the Captain.

▧ ✛ ▧

Three days later, Gulliver finished signing his name with a flourish. He stood back and eyed the addition he had made to the King's edict, which a dagger still pinned to the outpost gate.

"Come, my Squire," a knight called to him from astride a spirited charger. "Now that you have been assigned to me, I must improve your swordsmanship."

Gulliver grinned. "Immediately, Charity Joy. I am eager to learn."

He took one last look at the edict. Beneath the last rule, he had written, "If you have any questions, ask me. Signed, Gulliver Lamm, Squire." And beneath that were nailed twenty-four lizard-like hides for all the world to see.

The Secret Chamber

I N THE pre-dawn twilight, the mist from the falls chilled the young knight's face and hands. Drops gathered in his uncut brown hair, and on the links of his chain mail; but it would take much more than cold to keep him from his secret meeting. He pushed through the brambles and wild ivy beside the stream to hidden stone stairs, cut into the mountain beside the falls, and climbed them.

The stairs ended in a secret chamber of rock, etched centuries ago by the flow of the Crystal Stream, and now hidden behind a curtain of water. For the entire eastern wall of the alcove was open, so that the knight could see the back of the waterfall. The plash and play of the water cascading into the stream below echoed in the room, which smelled of wet stone.

"You are well met, young knight," a man's voice resounded in the rock chamber.

The knight turned and saw, seated on a bench-shaped boulder, the Captain of the Host, deep-chested and strong of arm. The Captain's flowing black hair, shot through with white, was graced by a circlet of gold, for he was also the Prince of the Realm.

The knight broke into a grin. "It matters not how early I attend our secret rendezvous; you are always here first, waiting." His voice reverberated from the rock, too. "Have you no other matters to attend to?"

The Captain smiled back. "None more important." He removed his helmet from another stone bench nearby, and the young knight sat. As they did every morning, they began talking of matters both small and great.

But today, after the knight had unburdened his heart, the Captain turned grave.

"Gone are the days when you were Gulliver, a squire," he said. "It has been two summers since I named you Denemir—'Faithful One'— and you became a knight. You have served well. Yet all your missions have been in Evermore, where the High King is openly acknowledged."

Denemir tried to contain his excitement. He could tell the Captain needed him.

"There is one known to me," the Captain continued with saddened eyes, "whose need is desperate. His heart longs for everything that Evermore has and is. But because he lives where the Pretender claims rule, he is deceived, and thinks Evermore is a lying dream."

"We must go to him," Denemir breathed. "But if he dwells in Ssenkrad, where men know things backwards if they know anything at all, how can he ever know the King aright?"

"One glimpse of my Father's glory is all he needs. His heart will tell him the rest. Will you show him?"

Denemir slipped from the stone seat and knelt. "I go wherever you send me, liege."

"I do not send you lightly, Faithful One." The Captain's blue eyes looked deep into Denemir. For many seconds, the only sound was the foaming water outside. The Captain continued, "Your heart is right, but you have little experience. Such a journey could cost your life. I release you to stay here if you wish. I will not think less of you."

Sir Lamm returned the Captain's gaze. "If you tell me to go," he said, "then I know there must be a way I can succeed."

The Captain laughed. "Such faith gladdens my heart," he said. "You are right. I will give you all you need to do this thing; and in doing, you will gain the experience you lack.

"The first thing you need is my counsel. Listen. In Ssenkrad, they disavow any knowledge of the High King. Because their thinking begins with this lie, all else is twisted, even from those whose intentions are not evil. You need not fear them; but do not walk in their counsel, or sit in the seat of the scornful.

"Next, the Pretender will sense your presence as soon as you cross the borders he claims as his. He will try you sorely. But you will have help: you may take anyone from my army whose love calls them to your aid. And I will be ever near, even in Ssenkrad, in guises new to you."

"But to whom do you send me?" asked Denemir. "And

how will I know him?"

"He lives near Castle Carousal," replied the Captain, "and spends much time at its fair. But when you first see him, he will be sitting alone, on a fallen pine, gazing upon that which is gray yet holds all colors. Can you remember this?"

"I know the Castle, for you rescued me from there. And I can remember what you say. But I do not understand it."

"The meaning will reveal itself. Now then." The Captain stood and shrugged off his scarlet cloak. Denemir now saw the Captain's tabard, a sleeveless shirt that hung, front and back, to his knees. Denemir's was identical, displaying a golden lion rampant upon a royal blue field, with a dozen six-pointed stars. But the Captain's tabard was gathered at the waist with a finely crafted leather belt having a large gold buckle, much superior to the piece of rope that gathered Denemir's.

The Captain removed the belt. "Hold this," he ordered, thrusting it into Denemir's bewildered hands.

He then pulled the tabard over his head, revealing his silver breastplate. The Captain unbuckled it. As he did so, the plain linen jerkin beneath it pulled up, briefly exposing a long and cruel scar in the Captain's side. The Captain handed the breastplate to the mystified knight.

Soon the knight had, piled in his arms, the Captain's own shield, shoes, helmet, belt, and breastplate. "Now," the barefoot Captain ordered, "put on my armor."

"Nay!" Denemir gasped. "I am not worthy to take—"

The Captain interrupted firmly. "I never send a knight to

battle without armor. Wear them."

The knight rose and complied. Soon he stood encased in shining silver, which seemed to glow in the half-light of the alcove. "My Lord!" Denemir exclaimed. "You are much larger than my slender frame, and yet—it fits! This is magic indeed!"

The Captain smiled. "It is far beyond magic; farther than words can express. The source of the armor's power is pure. Let us say that there is a virtue upon it."

Denemir stared down at himself in amazement. He rapped his gloved knuckles against the breastplate. "It is light as a whisper, but hard as diamond!"

"Even more: outside of Evermore, the armor is invisible. At times you will nearly forget you have it on—but you must not. Do not remove it while you are on your mission. Wear it. Wear *all* of it."

Denemir knelt and kissed the Captain's hand. "You are too generous. Among men there is no Prince like you."

The Captain laughed again. "To give recklessly is my delight. And thus, I would now give you my blessing."

Denemir bowed his head and knelt. He felt the Captain's hand rest upon his scalp. He closed his eyes.

"Now, fell and shining one," the Captain said, "I enable you to free the prisoners of darkness. I empower you against the Enemy. Watch for him, and he cannot harm you. Obey me, and he will fear you. Resist him, and he will flee you. In time of need, call on your Captain, and I will come to you. Before you begin, I give you victory. Go and take it."

At each sentence, Denemir's heart swelled. And then, even with his eyes closed, he felt another presence in the secret chamber. Unannounced, unheard, the High King himself had stolen into the chamber and now stood behind the kneeling knight. The King rested his hand upon his Son's. The King said only three words: "Remember my love."

At the sound of his voice, the rising sun struck the curtain of water with gold. Sensing the light against his eyelids, Denemir opened them, to see the light broken into a rainbow of colors that danced in the alcove. A chorus of lovely birdcalls swelled from outside to greet the dawn, like a choir rejoicing. And a sweet-smelling morning breeze bore a flurry of fresh-woken butterflies into the chamber, blue and purple and golden wings forming Nature's shimmering crown around the heads of the Son and the unseen King. Somehow, the Captain stood garbed in a new set of armor, as if he had never given away his own.

Glory filled Denemir's soul. *Remember?* he thought. *How could I forget the happiest moment of my life?*

◈ ✢ ◈

Denemir and Talitha's bursts of laughter echoed among the mighty trees of the gentle woodland slope. "Cease, Rannulf!" Denemir pleaded, wiping tears away. "We have nearly laughed ourselves to a halt!"

"Don't stop him!" Talitha begged. "I would hear how it ends!" The lithe redhead pushed her quiver's shoulder-strap back into place, and shifted her pack to where it had been before laughter convulsed her. Her chain mail glittered in a leaf-filtered sunbeam. "Thus," she prodded.

Because Rannulf was from the North, the brawny young knight's hair grew twice as fast as the lowlanders'. It had reached his waist in dense black waves before he grew so tired of it that he hacked it off with a sharp rock. Now short, thick, and apparently possessed of its own mind, his hair shot out in all directions from under his horned helmet. "Thus," he resumed, "the runaway cart crashed into Tanner John's stone fence, and pitched me straight into his pit!"

Denemir and Talitha guffawed. Tanners soaked leather in a mixture of formaldehyde, tree pulp, and animal offal to lighten its color. "Nothing stinks worse than the tanner's bath!" Talitha exclaimed.

"Except Rannulf's singing," Denemir grinned.

Rannulf paid Denemir with a blow to the shoulder. "'But," Rannulf finished, "you have not truly smelt the tanner's bath until it has bleached your own hide!"

The two stared at Rannulf in disbelief for a moment. Then the thought of the ruddy-faced, burly warrior, so fierce in battle, sitting dazed in a tanner's pit as the bath bleached him pale, threw them into laughter again.

"At the time, I laughed not!" Rannulf protested. "It burned like liquid fire! It took me three moons to return to my usual noble color. But . . ." The fighter paused, then shrugged his broad shoulders, causing the mace at his belt to clank against his breastplate. "That was *before*. I learned to laugh at misfortunes after I met the King!"

Talitha shook her long red locks. "I can almost smell it now," she said. Then she stopped in her tracks, and a frown replaced her smile. "Indeed, I *can* smell it now! How far are we from Ssenkrad?"

"This is our eighth march," Denemir answered. "We are close."

Talitha ran up the path to the top of the rise they had been climbing. She looked ahead, then beckoned to them.

Denemir and Rannulf topped the rise, and gazed into the valley below. "We are not close," Rannulf said. All trace of humor had left his voice. "We are there."

The sweet woodlands of Evermore ended where the three stood. Below and for many miles ahead lay the dead forests of Ssenkrad. Pines, once evergreen, stood black, twisted, and barren, jutting up like burnt bones from the ashes. The scorched ground bore little undergrowth, except for thorns and straggly vines. No birdcalls graced the air. A heavy, filthy mist twined like tentacles among the trees.

Rannulf was the first to take a step forward. Instantly, his armor vanished. Denemir murmured in surprise, then remembered the Captain's words. He began descending the slope. His armor disappeared, too, but a rap on the breastplate proved it was still there.

As they followed Rannulf, the light grew dim though the sun rode high. The bilious sky, turned twilight with foul smoke, seemed to press on them. "Surely there has been a grievous fire in this forest!" Talitha said, gazing around with distaste.

"Nay," Denemir said heavily. "It has been choked to death by the reek of yon Pits." He pointed ahead. At the base of the slope, all along the border between the two kingdoms, yawned huge chasms. They stretched longer than jousting fields, and wider than men can jump. The vines and thorns dangled down into them. Chill clouds of fume and vapor rose up from them. "They are bottomless. Many an unwary traveler trying to escape Ssenkrad has slipped in the tangling vines, and been pulled into the Pits of Despair to fall forever. We must find a path between them."

They walked deeper into the poisoned forest. There were no birdcalls. Only unseen slitherings and hisses broke the silence.

Near one of the Pits, they stopped. "Scout for a way around," Denemir said. "But beware the edge. Do not draw too near."

As Rannulf and Talitha separated, Denemir tried to peer into the chasm. An acrid, cold draft rose from it, stinging his eyes, blinding him. He blinked hard, repeatedly. When his vision cleared, he could no longer see his companions through the mist.

Before he could call to them, Denemir became aware of a huge, silent man to his left, obscured by the floating haze. Unaccountably, fear washed over the knight. "Who goes there?" he cried out.

A foul gust of air ripped the haze aside. Now Denemir could see it was no man. The creature, manlike but nine feet tall, spread leathery bat wings and flapped closer. Dried blood smeared its black armor. A spiked helm hid its face, but merciless, deadly eyes shone through the visor. The eyes looked Denemir up and down, coldly.

Despite himself, the young knight took a step back. His hand went to his sword hilt. Denying his dread, he demanded, "Name yourself!"

A cold, rasping voice echoed from the helmet, and a frigid vapor with it. "I am the Captain of Despair." The being flexed scaly, snakelike fingers that ended in talons. "You have entered my domain. Thus, you are mine."

Anger strengthened Denemir. "Nay, vile pretender! The true King purchased back all kingdoms with his own Son. You rule nothing."

"Look about," Despair whispered. "Does it look as though your so-called King rules here? This land is mine. I do not permit your mission."

"Then I defy you," Denemir proclaimed.

Despair laughed. "State your puny defiance!" the cold voice rasped. "But know you this. I never tire. I never give in. I am more patient than you. I am older than you. I am stronger than you. Sooner or later," Despair breathed intensely, and the eyes glowed from the visor with an infernal light, "I *will* have my way."

Denemir gulped. He began to believe Despair.

Arctic breath carried the voice once again, freezing Denemir. "I will prove who rules here," it said. Before Denemir could move, Despair pounced heavily on him. Effortlessly, the black captain lifted the knight overhead, and hurled him into the bottomless Pit of Despair.

Belt and Breastplate

URPRISE SEIZED Denemir so firmly that he had no time to cry out. One moment he was defying the Black Captain; the next, he was tumbling deeper and deeper into the bottomless Pit of Despair.

The vines and thorns dangling into the Pit lashed at him as he plummeted. He flailed in utter horror, grabbing at the vines; but each time he snatched at them, their waxy coating slid through his grasp, and he fell into deeper darkness.

Panic had nearly possessed Denemir when he felt a jolting tug at his waist, and an answering sharp pain in his lower back. Suddenly he was flying up. A moment later, he fell a few feet again, and stopped. He seemed to be suspended in mid-air. Slowly, he began to spin.

His heart battered at his rib cage like a lunatic determined to escape his cell. What had stopped him? Why wasn't he falling?

He looked down. His feet dangled in mid-air. Other than that, darkness and mists obscured whatever was below.

He looked up. The mouth of the Pit, which had yawned

so large from up above, looked like a crack of daylight from this far below. The crack appeared to spin in lazy circles. Leading from it, all the way down to him, was a vine.

Suddenly he realized what had stopped him. With exaggerated caution, he peeked downward again. Sure enough— a thorn on the vine had snagged the buckle of the huge Belt of Truth, which Denemir's Captain had given him. That was what had stopped him. The belt emanated a subtle golden glow in the gloom.

Now that he understood, Denemir reacted quickly. He grasped the vine with both hands, put his feet together, and swung them: left, then right, then left. Soon he had his body swinging in broader and broader arcs, so that he could touch either side of the Pit. Timing it carefully, he pulled himself up, off the thorn that had snagged him. When he was at the peak of the left swing, he let go of the vine and landed lightly on a ledge in the Pit's rough wall.

Denemir paused to catch his breath. His armor had nearly fallen off during his plunge. As he set it firmly back in place, his mind raced. He was out of immediate danger. But how could he get out of the Pit? The few vines that reached him were too slender to support his weight, and too slippery to hang onto. The wall of the Pit offered very few footholds, and those were of crumbling sandstone.

Somehow, Denemir had not perished—this time. But he was badly frightened. Denemir's Captain had promised that if the knights resisted the enemy, the enemy would flee. Yet the Black Captain's surprise attack would have succeeded, if Denemir hadn't benefited from this lucky coincidence—

At that, the young knight caught himself, and laughed in the dark. Experience had taught him that when serving the King, there was no such thing as coincidence. In fact, this kind of improbable, beyond-the-last-minute rescue was just like the King. If Despair had yet to flee, then Denemir must not be done resisting him.

For Despair's words held very little truth. Yes, Despair was older and stronger and larger than Denemir. But the truth was, Denemir had strength beyond his own to rely upon.

As this thought came to him, his belt's golden glow brightened.

And, Denemir realized, Despair *would* give up after he had been beaten enough times. Denemir's Captain had promised as much. He had blessed the young knight with victory.

This battle was not yet done.

While the young knight's heart filled with courage, the belt's glow swelled until it enveloped him. His fear had vanished. In its place were memories of all the times the Captain of the Host's words had proven true.

With a start, he noticed the walls of the Pit floating past. Denemir looked down, and laughed again. His Captain had told him there was a virtue on this armor. Now, as he watched, the Belt of Truth lifted him out of the Pit of Despair. He was floating up!

This fresh proof of the Captain's power emboldened

Denemir. Pleased to find that his sword had not fallen from him in the plunge, he drew it. Its keen edge caught the light from above, and reflected it into the Pit. As he floated higher, the light grew stronger.

Now the lip of the Pit drew near and he could hear sounds of battle. From above came fierce cries, the angry rush of an arrow through the air, and the clank of sword on shield.

As his face rose out of the Pit, Denemir's eyes searched the mist for the source of the sounds. There—the Captain of Despair fought with Rannulf as Talitha waited, bow drawn, for a chance to send another shaft into the enemy.

With a frightening roar, Despair swung an obsidian sword at Rannulf and landed an awful blow. Rannulf blocked it with his Shield of Faith, but the force of it knocked him to his knees. As Despair reared back to deliver a two-handed death blow, Talitha sped one shaft, then a second, into joints of Despair's black armor.

The evil Captain roared, more from anger than from pain. Four arrows stuck out of him at various places. He swept one powerful arm across the arrows, snapping them off like dried twigs. But as he lifted his sword again, he now faced an extra fighter.

When Despair saw Denemir, a surprised puff of vapor escaped his visor.

Denemir's smile was grim. "The King has lifted me out of your slimy pit, and set my feet on a rock," he rebuked his enemy. "Now you will be put to shame and confusion!"

Despair faltered. Denemir attacked, denting the black armor with stroke after stroke from his sword. Then Rannulf's whirling mace hit Despair so mightily that the black helmet split open.

Despair's bat-like wings whipped open and pulled him back and up, out of their reach. Chill vapor poured from the cleft in his helmet. He hovered over them, as if uncertain what to do.

An arrow hissed past Denemir into one of Despair's wings. That seemed to decide the Black Captain. "When you are less vigilant," he rasped at them, "your throats will feel my talons!" Then he swooped into the Pit, vanishing in subterranean shadows far below.

Denemir felt like collapsing to the ground in relief, but remained standing. "You both fought well," he panted.

"It did not take long for the rulers of Ssenkrad to note our presence," Rannulf said, hooking his mace back to his belt.

Talitha joined them, shouldering her bow. "And I am glad you are well," she told Denemir. "We looked for you, but found a foe."

"I will explain, but far from these stinking Pits," Denemir replied. "You found a way around them? Then lead me out of here. Despair has fled for now, but will return with help from his legion."

"We must move with great speed to escape this scorched forest before nightfall," Rannulf responded. "This way." He strode away at a brisk pace.

The others followed. Denemir spared one last glance back at the Pits. The mist made him uncertain, but he thought he glimpsed the Captain of Despair, hovering in the fumes, watching.

◈ ✛ ◈

A small cooking fire crackled merrily in the dusk, with a make-shift spit prepared above it, when Talitha returned to the clearing with a brace of quail. "These would not make a meal for even one of us," she observed as she laid them by the fire, "but they may help our provisions to last. They were all I could find in this dying land."

Denemir began cleaning the quail. "Scant it may be," he commented, "but it is far better than the ashen forest offered. I am glad it is miles behind us."

Talitha sat on a stump, sighed, and removed her pack, bow, and quiver. "Today's was a long and hard march. Do you reckon us safe?"

Denemir's knife paused as he surveyed the bare, stunted trees that surrounded the clearing, choked by nettles and weeds, blanketed in shadow. "This is a dry and weary land," he said. "Without the King's help, we are safe nowhere."

"But with the King's help, we are safe anywhere!" came a deep, cheerful voice. Rannulf sauntered into the clearing. Even in the half-light, they could see his hair was wet.

"Did you enjoy your swim?" Talitha, massaging one weary foot, asked.

"Most delightsome!" Rannulf responded. "There are

ponds of refreshing even in Ssenkrad!" He sniffed, as if just noticing the fire. "When do we eat?"

"It will be awhile for the quails," Denemir admitted. "But we can eat the first course." From his pack, he brought out a supply of honeyed daybread from the King's kitchens. Carefully breaking it apart, he provided each knight with a ration.

By now darkness had fallen, but the fire cheered the knights. They sat around it, munching the daybread, talking and laughing.

Finally Denemir turned the spit a final time. Hot grease dripped and sizzled. "Done to perfection!" he announced triumphantly, and swiftly removed the meat.

Denemir passed a portion to Rannulf, but the burly knight sat gazing at nothing, as if lost in thought. Denemir waved the platter before Rannulf's face. No response.

"Hoy!" Talitha called. "If it pleases you not, speak, and I will eat it!"

Rannulf shook his head as if coming to, noticed the proffered plate for the first time, and seized it. "I thank you," he said, and bit into a drumstick.

"Are you well?" Denemir asked.

"Fine, fine," Rannulf said with his mouth full. He waved the drumstick in the air. "Merely thinking."

"The last time you had a thought," Talitha teased, "it perished of loneliness!"

The others laughed, and Rannulf lobbed a bone toward her. More banter followed, but most of the exchanges were between Denemir and Talitha. Rannulf, normally long-winded, lapsed into longer silences. His round face grew less animated.

The conversation lagged again. Denemir tossed a fresh branch on the fire. Sparks flew up, throwing a golden glare on Rannulf's face. His expression was undeniably sad.

"Rannulf," Denemir urged softly. "What troubles you?"

Rannulf swallowed and hesitated. "I . . . it was a near fight today."

"Aye," Denemir agreed. "But for a bruise on your shield arm, though, we are all untouched. The King triumphed!"

"But you almost died!" Rannulf began bluntly. Then he caught himself. "No, you are right. We won." Speaking to the fire, or perhaps to himself, he repeated, "We won."

Denemir shot a glance at Talitha, who frowned back in concern. The fire popped once in the gloomy silence.

"It's just . . ." Rannulf began, and stopped. After a moment, he said, "How do we know we can keep winning?"

"Because of the Captain's promise," Denemir said.

"Despair will be back," Rannulf continued, as if he hadn't heard Denemir. "Yes, the King will try to help us. But what if I stumble during the fight? Or what if the King has given me an instruction that I've forgotten? All could be lost!" Agitated, he stared at the other two. In the firelight, they could see he was sweating.

"Surely it is your weariness speaking!" Talitha answered. "You are the bravest fighter I've seen. These could not be your words!"

"Think, lass!" Rannulf retorted, now growing angry. "We are nine days' march from the Citadel, in a land where no one acknowledges the King. We are alone out here, against a devious foe that does not tire!"

"Calm yourself—" Denemir began.

"Do you not understand?" Rannulf barked. He dashed his platter to the ground, and jumped to his feet. "Am I the only one who sees the danger we are in? We are overmatched! To survive, I must be perfect! Yet I cannot be perfect! Sooner or later, our enemy will take me!"

Rannulf paced restlessly. "You two will be safe!" he insisted. Jabbing a finger at each of them in turn, he said, "You are beautiful and sweet. And you know the Captain better than we two. But Rannulf, foolish, ugly, fat Rannulf, is another story! I am sinful and gross. The King forgave me once, but I have sinned many times since then. I deserve to perish here. He will not help me like he helps you, because I am not worthy!"

The other two rose slowly. "Friend—" Denemir began.

With a cry of anguish, Rannulf spun and bolted. Denemir, half expecting it, leaped onto his friend and bore him to the ground. Rannulf twisted, trying to get free, as Denemir tried to hold him. They rolled dangerously close to the fire.

Rannulf broke away. He jumped up. Denemir lunged for him, snagging only Rannulf's jerkin. Rannulf spun, and the sound of tearing cloth filled the clearing. Both men froze in horror.

Revealed in the orange firelight, attached under Rannulf's torn jerkin and over his heart, a huge leech sucked at his chest. It was fat, large as Rannulf's fist, and gorged on Rannulf's blood.

Talitha broke the silence first. "You tore his jerkin," she murmured. "But that means . . ."

It hit Denemir. "You are not wearing your breastplate!"

"I . . . I . . ." Rannulf gulped. "I took it off to swim. My helmet is with it. They are invisible, and I forgot!" All fight gone, his eyes pleaded with them. "Help me!"

Together, they brought him back to the fire and seated him. Talitha, wiser in woodlore than the others, inspected the leech. "It is a Leech of Self-Doubt," she concluded. "From the pond. You cannot handle it. Either his chest will tear open, or it will attach itself to you." She turned solemn brown eyes upon Denemir. "You must cut it away with your sword."

"So near his heart?" Denemir asked. "One slip and I could slay him!"

"You see his condition," Talitha answered soberly. "The longer it drinks from him, the worse he will get. By morning, he could die."

Denemir absorbed this, then nodded once. "So we must risk it." The drawing of his sword rang into the night air. "Can you hold him?"

"I will try." Talitha moved behind Rannulf, pulling his arms back. "You must hold very still, brother."

Rannulf did not answer at first. His eyes were fixed on

the sword, which Denemir held in the flame, to sterilize. Finally, Rannulf said, "Do it."

Denemir pulled the sword from the fire. The blade glowed a dull red, and the stars above it shimmered.

Holding the Sword of the Spirit with both hands, he poised it within an inch of the leech. Denemir held Rannulf's gaze. "I will hurt you as little as I can," Denemir said. "I wield this blade in love, and do not savor using it on you."

Rannulf inhaled deeply, then held his breath. Through gritted teeth, he repeated, "Do it."

11

An Exceedingly Helpful Madman

THE RED-HOT sword tip hovered near the slimy leech on Rannulf's chest, but instead of shrinking away, the leech swallowed faster. Denemir urged, "Understand this, Rannulf. Without the Breastplate of Righteousness, you feel your unworthiness. But you did not receive a spirit that makes you a slave again to fear. You received the Spirit of sonship. The High King is a loving Father to you now."

A gust of wind fanned the campfire. In its rising orange glow, he strengthened his grip on the sword so that he could hold it perfectly steady. The trick would be to kill the bloodsucker without wounding Rannulf further. He glanced at Talitha, who held Rannulf's arms back and braced him so he was still. She nodded that she was ready.

Denemir gauged the force of the blow, then stabbed the parasite. Its tough hide resisted the sword for a moment, then punctured. Blood began to squirt. Rannulf inhaled sharply through clenched teeth.

Denemir cried, "Your worthiness matters not, Rannulf.

You are accepted in the Beloved! Now die, lying leech!" He stabbed again. This time the parasite let out a thin, shrill screech, and plopped to the ground. Quickly Denemir stepped on it, grinding its head under the heel of his shoe.

Where the bloodsucker had latched onto Rannulf's chest, blood flowed freely from a welt. Denemir hesitated, then placed the flat of the red-hot blade over the wound. Rannulf screamed and struggled to get away. There was the sound and smell of sizzling, dying flesh. Talitha held on with all her might. Denemir continued pressing the sword home until Rannulf's scream died to a whimper, and he ceased struggling.

Denemir removed the sword. There was no more welt and no more blood. In their place, tender, new, pink skin formed the shape of the sword tip over his heart. Talitha and Rannulf both gasped in wonder. Rannulf collapsed against Talitha, who gently laid him down.

Talitha fetched cool water and poured it over Rannulf's wound. "The sword's virtue has begun his healing well," she said, "but it is not finished."

Using the blade, Denemir flicked the leech's carcass into the sizzling fire. "We must return to the place where he lost his breastplate and find it. Until he replaces it, the burn will ache, and he will have no protection against further parasites."

"He has lost much blood," Talitha worried. "He is weak."

"And will be for some days," Denemir replied as he sheathed his sword. "Yet we cannot risk any other course.

Come, we must help him to the pond."

Soon they each had one of Rannulf's arms over their shoulders. His companions bore most of his weight. "Can you walk?" Denemir inquired anxiously.

Rannulf answered weakly, "Go."

They began hobbling toward the pond. "I am sorry I hurt you," Denemir said. "There was no other way."

"You saved my life," Rannulf murmured. Beads of perspiration still dotted his brow, but he forced a smile as he limped into the night. "Faithful are the wounds of a friend."

✤

By twilight the next day, with the armor recovered and Rannulf hobbling under his own power, they spied a small village through the trees.

Closer inspection proved it was hardly a village at all, but a few buildings which had sprung up around a crossroads. An inn, a provisions merchant, and the cottages of the people who ran them clustered around an intersection where dirt roads split off in three directions.

The trio stood in the intersection and eyed the sizable log inn. A bushy thatched roof nearly hid the sign hanging in front. It pictured a pompous rooster with steel spurs strapped to its legs. "The Fighting Cock," Talitha read.

"Dare we stay here?" Denemir wondered.

"It will be dark soon," Talitha reminded them. "And despite our friend's brave efforts, I think a bed would do him well."

Denemir glanced at Rannulf. The burly knight's pale complexion belied his resolute expression. He wavered as he stood. "Very well," Denemir agreed. "But we are inexperienced with these people, so keep your defenses ready."

As Denemir tugged open the inn's oak door, shouting and harsh laughter poured out. The tavern sounded full. "So I says to her," one old man was bellowing, "I'll show ye what a wench *should* do with it!" The patrons bellowed coarse approval, and banged mugs on tables.

The knights entered, blinking in the sudden gloom. First Denemir noticed the mingled odors of many bodies, much ale, and smoking lamp wicks stuffed into a closed room. Then he noticed that the laughter had suddenly died away. Finally his eyes adjusted to the dim lighting, and he found that in this low-beamed room, filled with crude wooden benches and tables and shadows, every person in the crowd stared silently at the knights and their tabards.

"Good eventide," Denemir bade them. Feeling the eyes upon him, he led his companions to an empty table in the farthest corner from the fireplace.

As they sat, the proprietor, a tall, heavyset man with stringy hair and a filthy apron, sauntered up to them. He grunted, "Ale?"

"Water," Denemir answered. Pointing at Rannulf, "Plenty for him. And food."

Instead of bustling away to comply, the man glowered at them. "Most folks prefer ale."

"I am sure it is fine ale. Water, please."

Without answering, the proprietor lumbered away.

Denemir glanced around and saw that everyone still stared at them. Most of the room was filled with Ssenkradian soldiers, who had apparently ended their day's march here.

Talitha whispered, "Mayhap we should have accepted the ale, without drinking it."

Rannulf said in an undertone, "Mayhap we should leave."

From the back of the common room, a soldier stood. He paced deliberately toward the knights, and stopped in front of them. He had oily dark hair and a mustache. "You are not from Ssenkrad," he said in a nasal voice.

Though he stood shorter than most of the soldiers, his tabard bore many pins and medals. Denemir guessed they indicated high rank. He resolved to treat this man carefully. "No, but we bear good will toward all Ssenkradians," Denemir answered. Rannulf fidgeted, annoyed by the challenge and the cautious response.

"'Good will,'" the officer repeated skeptically. He removed a glove and slapped it across his palm. "How can that be, when you wear the tabard of a rival kingdom?"

Rannulf's expression darkened, but Denemir responded, "The King of Evermore wants only abundant life for all of you."

To his surprise, the room erupted into laughter. "You actually believe in a King in Evermore?" the officer jeered. "Tell me," and here he winked at the room, "have you ever *seen* your King?"

"I know Him well . . ." Denemir began, but Rannulf interrupted by jumping to his feet.

"Your mockery does not frighten us," Rannulf stated. "We are the King's knights, and if you trouble us, you will suffer the King's wrath. Then you, too, will believe in the King—although a trifle too late." He glared a challenge at the officer, who merely smiled.

"That sounds more like Evermore," he replied coolly. "Not that twaddle about your so-called King wanting our good."

Rannulf growled and reached for his mace. Instantly the room bristled with short swords and javelins. Rannulf froze, with Denemir's hand staying his arm.

"As usual, you Evermorons proclaim 'good will,' but act out malice," the officer sighed. "That is why Ssenkradian soldiers find you insignificant." He turned to the room and announced, "These striplings, who fancy themselves our rivals, bore me. If any of you would have some idle fun, I will not stop you." He strutted back to his table.

One by one, six soldiers rose from the crowd, evil grins upon their faces. They wielded an assortment of weapons: pikes, swords, cudgels, and knives. As they advanced upon the trio, Denemir and Talitha stood. "We mean you no harm," Denemir protested. "Do we, Rannulf?" Under the table, he kicked his friend.

"Um, indeed," Rannulf said. "Forgive my hasty speech. Instead of fighting, why not hear more of our King? You'd better, or else! Ow! I mean, or not. That is to say . . ." He trailed off, tongue-tied.

The men arrayed themselves into a war party. When only the wooden table separated the two factions, Denemir drew his sword, and Talitha strung an arrow. Someone from the back hurled a mug at them, which dashed to pieces against Denemir's invisible breastplate.

"Once I tear your arm off," a large soldier with a cudgel growled, "I will use it to beat your friends to death. Defend yourself—if you can."

The knights raised their weapons.

Suddenly a blast of off-key music filled the room. With a whoop and a yelp, a white-bearded man dressed in countless strips of multi-colored cloth leaped onto the table between the opponents. Pumping a worn, tiny accordion madly, he spun into a whirling jig and sang,

> *Am I a musician, a loon, or a magician?*
> *To answer your suspicions, I say I am superior!*
> *The soul of my mission is a comic exhibition.*
> *I have the disposition of a prominent posterior!*

With that, he squatted and let loose an enormous, ripping flatulence. As the drunken soldiers burst into surprised laughter, the old man poked his huge nose next to Denemir's and hissed, "Second floor, second room—*go!*" He immediately launched into another verse.

Denemir didn't pause to listen. "This way!" he urged his

friends. They scurried past the armed party which, between the ale they had already consumed and their helpless guffaws, quite ignored the knights. He urged them through the doorway into the kitchen. His final glance back at the room revealed that the madman had fallen on the table and was trying to pick himself up by his own nose. His nose stretched impossibly long until it snapped in two. As the soldiers slapped each other's backs in mirth, Denemir realized the man had been wearing flesh-colored putty. Ignoring the cries of the cook, he pushed the others through the kitchen into the courtyard beyond.

"Second floor," Denemir urged. He surveyed the twilit yard and the stables and found the stairs. They rushed up them, hurried into the second room they came to, and slammed and barred the door.

"Who—or what—was that?" Talitha panted.

"An exceedingly helpful madman, " Denemir said. "He probably saved our lives."

Turning on Rannulf, Talitha added, "And what did you think you were doing?"

"I am gravely sorry," Rannulf blushed. "I did not think at all. I wanted to prove to that insolent little officer that we are not ashamed of our King."

"Next time, temper your boldness with wisdom," Denemir suggested ruefully. "Nonetheless, you are readily forgiven." He examined the room. It contained a pair of straw beds, a wooden table, and a chair. Upon the table stood a clay pitcher full of water, and a bowl. A window looked out over the stables. A side door led to a smaller chamber, adjoined to their room and containing a single small bed. "We are safe here for the night. We can bar the door, shutter the window, and sleep peacefully. There is even a chamber for Talitha's privacy."

Behind him sounded the thud of something fallen. He turned and found Rannulf on the floor, shaking his head dazedly.

Talitha helped Rannulf into a bed. She brought the pitcher to him and let him drink deeply. "His lost blood did not aid his flight. He must rest tonight," she told Denemir.

Rannulf insisted wearily from the bed, "One mighty meal will set me straight."

"We must lie low for now," Denemir said. "When the soldiers have drunk themselves into a stupor, I will buy us some food. Until then, here is some daybread."

Quite some time later, with the stars high in the sky, knuckles rapped at the door. "Who goes there?" called Denemir.

Ragged accordion notes answered.

Denemir unbarred the door and admitted the white-bearded man, who balanced platters of food on both arms. The concertina, clutched between his knees, wheezed as he tiptoed in. He deposited a few of the plates on the table, then passed the others to Rannulf, Talitha, and Denemir.

Rannulf expressed his gratefulness by tearing into the roasted chicken. Talitha said, "We thank you most kindly. You have saved us twice in one evening, yet we do not know your name!"

The old man bowed happily. In a surprisingly resonant voice, he said, "I am Teller!" He twirled lightly and ended in a performer's pose, arms spread wide. The strips of cloth hanging from his shoulders whispered as he moved. Pulling the concertina from between his legs, he added, "And unlike most folks around here, I have nothing against the High King."

"Welcome words, which explain your many kindnesses," Denemir said around a mouthful of bread. "I also thank you for saving us." Pulling a leather pouch from his pack, he added, "We can pay for the food, plus some for your trouble, Teller."

He counted out five coins, which Teller accepted with a bow. His outstretched hand disappeared into the strange shredded cloak. Eyeing Rannulf, Teller said, "You have much to learn about Ssenkradian customs. Where are you bound?"

"To the land near Castle Carousal. Do you know it?"

"Right well! This is good news!" Bird calls and bells sounded from under the cloak. "My way takes me halfway to the Castle before I must turn aside. If you will escort an old peddler as far as our journey lies together, you will show more kindness than I have! Provide protection, and I will provide knowledge to ease your way. What say you?"

"Peddler?" Talitha asked. "What do you sell?"

"Life itself! Laughter and a sigh. Great heroes, grave danger, deeds noble and nefarious. Justice by the measure, mirth by the cupful, and love by the pound!"

The knights exchanged glances. Denemir said, "Do you support the King of Evermore?"

"I like what I have heard, but know little," Teller said. "I would learn more!"

"That, we would joyfully share!" Talitha cried.

Denemir asked the knights, "Are we of one mind, then?" When they nodded, he turned to Teller and said, "We accept!"

Teller laughed happily, and they struck hands to seal the bargain. His eyes sparkled, and his red and blue and yellow cloak rustled. "Until the morn, then," he cried. The spry old man jumped onto the empty bed, did a back flip off it, and bounced to the door. He was gone before the knights had recovered from their surprise.

Spying some objects near the door, Denemir picked them up. They were his five coins and a note. He read aloud, " 'In exchange for kindliness, I never will purloin; you've paid me by the way the soldiers showered me with coin. Teller.' Fie! How did he do that?" There was a perplexed moment of silence. Then the knights began to laugh.

"Well," Rannulf grinned. "Surely we will not perish of boredom!"

The Invisible Helmet

A
T DAWN the next morning, Denemir, Rannulf, and Talitha crept through the shadows into The Fighting Cock's stable yard.

Teller had placed a bridle on his aged gray mare, and was walking toward the back of his bright red cart, when he noticed the knights across the dirt yard. "Hail and well met!" he boomed. Two startled finches fled from under his white beard. He was still shrouded in a cloak of many-colored strips.

Denemir winced. He had hoped to depart without being noticed by the Ssenkradian soldiers in the inn.

Reading the knight's expression, Teller called, "Do not fear the soldiers! They found their beds but an hour ago, far too drunk to pose a threat."

By now the three had crossed to the old peddler. Shaking long red hair from her eyes, Talitha smiled at him. "How would you know? Have you not found your own bed?"

"Bah! Old folk like me need little sleep, if any." Stepping on the hub of his cart wheel, he clambered into the driver's seat. His cart looked like a large box on wheels. Fancy gold lettering on the sides proclaimed, "TELLER of Tales. For Thine Amusement." "Now your friend, there"—he pointed at Rannulf, who was yawning and knuckling his eyes— "could hail from the northern Tartars, who sleep through the first six months of every year."

Talitha chuckled. "Is that true?"

"No," Teller answered gravely, "but I wish it were, because I tell it to everyone." His face looked so absurdly mournful that the knights broke into laughter.

Brightening, he said, "But I have a tale that *is* true. Do you know the story of the princess born blind, who did not know she was beauteous? And her suitor, a commoner?"

"I would hear it!" Talitha answered. She pulled her bow off her shoulder, then clambered onto the driver's bench next to Teller. "Born blind, you say?"

And Teller launched into his tale. It told of a great love, and of people persisting in good deeds though long unrewarded. The storyteller's skill surpassed anything Denemir had experienced. If the story included a bird, Teller perfectly reproduced the sound of the bird. He could imitate the wind, or sword clanking against shield, even a pack of wolves fighting. And Denemir could not tear his eyes from Teller, for the peddler punctuated his story with amusing faces, poignant gestures, and props which appeared from under his cloak. He imbued the princess with such virtue and tenderness, the suitor with such selfless devotion, that Denemir felt this was surely the greatest love of all time.

The tale ended happily, with the lovers married and the princess's sight restored. Touched, the knights stood speechless for many silent moments. Then brawny, dark-haired Rannulf breathed, "That is the noblest story I have ever heard."

Teller bowed humbly, then teased Rannulf. "That is Talitha's kind of tale. You would prefer the tale of the man who destroyed a dragon using only a mirror, a feather, and courage."

Before Rannulf could respond, Denemir laughed in embarrassment. "Your story was so magnificent," he said, "we have clean forgotten to leave!"

Talitha and Rannulf looked about themselves, as if surprised to find themselves still in The Fighting Cock's stable yard, the sun well up. They laughed at their own foolishness.

"Forgive a rambling old man," Teller begged. He gathered his reigns and shook them. "On, Lady Penumbra," he called, and the mare began walking slowly. With great creaking, the cart's wheels began to roll.

"Your mare's lofty name," Denemir said as he walked beside Teller's perch. "I suppose there is a story behind it?"

Teller laughed merrily. "My boy," he said, "there is a story behind *everything!*"

"But you were going to tell us of the dragon!" Rannulf said.

"There is time for all the stories," Teller answered. "We have all day!"

Amid plenty of good-natured arguing about what story

should be told when, and with much mirth, the cart turned at the crossroads and headed for Castle Carousal, many leagues ahead.

◈ ✛ ◈

As dusk approached, Denemir's head swam with countless stories he wanted to remember. There was the story of the knight who appeared to die justly in a joust, but was actually murdered—a scullery maid proved the opponent had poisoned the pre-tournament toast. There was the chilling tale of a fortune-teller who foresaw her own death; and in trying to prevent it, accidentally caused it. There were endless comic adventures of Rosencrantz and Guildenstern, two apprentice jesters who aspired to be knights but were outrageously dreadful at every job in the castle. And songs, a multitude of songs, all of them in awful taste but hilariously clever.

When Teller suggested they halt for the day, Denemir felt they had barely left The Fighting Cock. But a glance at the sinking sun proved nightfall approached. By Denemir's reckoning, the mare's slow gait had held them to half the miles the knights could readily travel in one day; but at least the time had passed quickly, and their spirits ran high. Besides, though Rannulf seemed stronger, they should not push his limits yet, not after all the blood he had lost to the Leech of Doubt.

The cart benefited them because they could park it anywhere and have instant shelter. And old Teller's stupendous supply of pots and pans made fixing meals a snap. Overall, the arrangement satisfied Denemir.

Around the after-dinner campfire, as the knights enjoyed the drowsy after-effects of a large meal, Teller blew smoke rings from his pipe—and smoke squares, and smoke triangles. "This High King of yours," the old man said. "Do you care for him greatly, or merely endure his reign?"

Sitting with his back against a tree trunk, Denemir answered, "We love Him with all our hearts."

Talitha nodded agreement, and Rannulf added, as he poked at the fire with a branch, "And His Son also, who saved my life."

Teller seemed intrigued. "A Prince? Saved your life?"

"And mine," Talitha added.

"And mine," Denemir grinned.

The old man shook his white head in wonder. "Imagine! A King and a Prince who save the lives of every one of their subjects!" He took a long pull on the pipe. Another thought struck him. He nearly disappeared in smoke as he asked, "Then why do people of Ssenkrad despise him?"

"Because they have made up their minds without knowing Him," Talitha answered.

"And we have been poor ambassadors of His great love," Denemir confessed.

"And the cruel Pretender King of Ssenkrad lies about him always," Rannulf added.

"Pretender King," Teller mused. "I know of a King so cruel that in the end the sun itself refused to shine on his kingdom."

Talitha laughed. "How could that be?"

"But there is only one real King," Rannulf interrupted. "The King over all Kings."

"This is merely a story," Teller justified. "No harm intended. It came about thusly: this King, who loved snakes, decided to proclaim the snakes royalty . . ."

Thus they whiled away the evening in fanciful stories. When Denemir awoke the next morning, he realized the knights had never told their stories of how the King saved them.

◈ ✛ ◈

Five days later, hot afternoon sun bore down on the travelers as they wound their way along one of Ssenkrad's dirt roads. It was Denemir's turn to perch in the driver's seat, next to Teller, who had just delighted the knights with another slapstick Rosencrantz and Guildenstern misadventure. Denemir relaxed and let Teller, who knew all the back roads, choose their way.

As the old man grinned down at the still-chuckling Rannulf and Talitha, who walked alongside the cart, his expression changed to one of curiosity. He asked, "Why do you hold one arm so strangely?"

"I am holding my helmet under my arm," Talitha answered. "It is too hot to wear, and I can hear you better without it."

Teller stared at the empty space between her hip and her arm, then burst into hearty laughter. From under his cloak came the blat and toot of several tiny horns. "Quite good!" he complimented. "For an instant, I believed you!"

"We do not jest," Rannulf said. "Our King gave us invisible helmets."

Teller chuckled again. "Then give them to me and watch me juggle them!"

Wordlessly, Denemir removed his helmet and placed it in Teller's lap.

The startled old man reigned Lady Penumbra to a halt. He stared at his own thighs. Hands trembling, he felt for the helmet. He hefted it, sensing its weight. He stared at Denemir, wide-eyed, then back at the helmet, which he still could not see. It looked as if he were holding his empty hands to show the size of a fish he once caught.

"The Helmet of Salvation has a virtue upon it," Denemir explained. "When I put it on, I can think more like my Captain. It protects not only my head, but my head's contents!"

Teller placed the helmet on his head, but it would not slip down. He tried adjusting it several ways, but it simply did not fit.

At length, he whispered, "Verily." Then he exclaimed, "I would never have believed this wonderful thing, had I not *not* seen it with my own eyes!" Shaking his head, Teller returned the helmet, picked up the reigns, and resumed their slow progress. "I have lived long and traveled well," he said. "But I have never seen its equal." After a moment, he muttered, "Invisible helmets. Reminds me of the Vortorian volunteer, who had two heads and lost them both. Have I told you of him? No? Well . . ."

Denemir settled back in his seat, ready to enjoy another story. He would wear the helmet in a moment. For now, he really could hear Teller better without it, and he relished the breeze fingering his hair.

⬧ ✝ ⬧

Three weeks after their first meeting with Teller, he declared the day Special, because they were due to arrive at his very best, highest-paying customer.

Today Rannulf sat with Teller, while Talitha walked near them. Denemir trudged behind the cart, lost in thought.

Something was bothering him.

He couldn't pinpoint what. His brain felt clouded. He tried to rehearse recent events in his mind, but he could only think of the baron's daughter who rebelled against her pre-arranged matrimony, claiming she would marry for love; and of the man who had come from far in the future, and told of marvelous carriages that rolled without horses.

Now bawdy lyrics were running through Denemir's mind, one of Teller's funniest songs. The knight shook his head to clear it. Somewhere, amidst the tales and songs, he had forgotten something.

A mighty *hallooo* sounded from ahead. Denemir hastened his pace. As he jogged out from behind the cart, he discovered it had stopped at a large two-story cottage having at least a dozen shuttered windows. Teller, standing high atop the cart, struck a theatrical pose and *halloooed* again.

The door of the cottage burst open. A buxom, dark-haired woman of perhaps forty ran out, waving and laughing. Teller leaped from the cart, completed two flips before hitting the ground, rolled through a somersault and bounced to his feet in the arms of the woman. He planted a loud kiss on her cheek.

"You rascal!" she said in mock fury. "No free samples! Girls! Girls, it's Teller!"

Shutters flew open and musical laughter filled the air. Three beautiful young women ran out the door, and more waved from the windows.

Denemir's eyes grew wide. These were not like the women of Evermore. These women wore no leggings, and no armor. In fact, they wore very little.

The giggling women surrounded Teller, embracing him, tugging at his cloak, playing with his hair and beard. He swatted some and kissed others, obviously delighted. "Madeline," he addressed the older woman, "it has been far too long since I visited your House of Delights!" So saying, he reached into his mouth and yanked out a huge bouquet of flowers, which he presented to her.

When the laughter died down, he said, "But you must meet my friends and escorts!" He turned to the knights. "Denemir, Talitha, Rannulf," he boomed cheerfully, "Welcome to Ssenkrad's finest brothel!"

Just as Teller had spoken, Denemir's wandering eye had crossed a window where a woman leaned out happily, wearing nothing.

That did it.

"We must flee!" he urged his startled friends. "Get your packs, your weapons. And in the King's name, put your helmets back on!"

As they scrambled to comply, Denemir added to Teller, "And you! I have given you more mind than ever I should. You do not intend mischief, but time long spent in your company somehow makes room for evil. We may meet another day, perhaps even sup together. But I will never journey with you again." With that, he spun on his heel, gathered his two friends, and bolted into the forest. His last glimpse through the trees revealed Teller dancing with the harlots, the knights already forgotten.

Denemir ran for miles before he allowed them to rest. "I beg your forgiveness," he panted. "I have played the fool."

"How . . . could we . . . have known?" Talitha gasped.

Rannulf, normally ruddy, looked pale. Bent over with his hands on his knees, he could only exclaim, "The King's knights . . . at a brothel!"

When their breath returned, Talitha unrolled a map from her pack and shared it with Denemir. After inspecting it, he declared, "Not only did we make slow progress, following his feeble mare and stopping at every village, but we have veered far from our course." He struck himself in the head. "I filled my head with nonsense, and forgot our mission. I forgot our Captain and our King. I am entirely unworthy to lead you." Angrily, he kicked at the ground.

"Nay," Rannulf said. "You did not force us. We agreed."

Denemir could not speak. Now, away from Teller's influence, he clearly remembered the Captain's words. A hurting heart waited out there, longing to know the King's glory. Its healing was delayed, its pain extended, for the sake of meaningless entertainment.

"We must make up for lost time," Denemir resolved. "Can you run, Rannulf?"

"Show me the proper direction," he said. "I will set the pace."

Talitha pointed north. They marched double-time, deeper and deeper into a vast forest. High above, branches increasingly blocked the sun until it seemed they ran in chilly dusk. Ferns and nettles hindered their progress. They found no paths except occasional deer runs.

When they had nearly exhausted themselves, they began noticing wolf tracks. Talitha knelt long enough to inspect them. "Fresh," she declared. "At least five in the pack. Larger than usual."

"If they find us, we cannot outrun them," Denemir panted. "We must move more slowly, to conserve energy and increase our stealth."

Upon the heels of his words came two noises. Strangely, the first sounded like a toddler, crying in the woods.

The second was the barking of the pack, frightfully near.

13
The Shepherd's Gifts

T HE CHILD'S cry again echoed off the tree trunks. It seemed to come from everywhere. Spurred by the sound of a helpless animal, the wolf barking doubled in volume.

"A babe in the woods," Talitha moaned in weariness. Denemir and Rannulf spun in circles, trying to spy the child among the pines, ferns, and brambles before the wolves did. Talitha's woodlore bested theirs, so when she went left, they followed.

Soon they could hear quiet sobbing. Denemir saw only a granite boulder so huge that the pine branches thirty feet above rested on it, covering it with brown needles. Stinging nettles obscured the bottom of the boulder. It sounded as if the rock itself were crying.

He squatted. Using his sword blade, he pushed the nettles aside. The bushes hid the fact that the boulder's base curved in deeply. Under this outcropping lay a very dirty, very frightened little girl, who stared out with wide, wet eyes. "Come here, little one," Denemir beckoned in soothing tones. The frightened toddler scrunched backward, deeper into her cubbyhole.

They heard the crack of dead branches stepped on by heavy animals. "Hurry!" Rannulf urged.

Hearing a snarl behind him, Denemir, in one motion, spun, stood, and positioned his sword.

A great gray wolf loped out of the brambles, fifty yards away. He froze and stared at them, baring his teeth. Rannulf, axe in hand, eyed him warily. Talitha nocked an arrow to her bow string and drew.

The wolf barked, startling them. They heard more branches snap, and four more wolves appeared, growling and snarling. The pack milled restlessly, shaggy and gaunt and looking very hungry. Their shoulders rose as high as Talitha's waist. Denemir, exhausted from a day's running, could hardly keep his eyes on the shifting gray shapes.

The wolves ranged back and forth, ever closer, cutting off any escape, coming within feet of the trio. The knights backed up against the boulder, desperately trying to guard their front and both flanks.

A wolf darted in and snapped at Rannulf's shins, testing for weakness. The axe cut the air, and had the wolf not been feinting, would have dealt a killing blow.

Suddenly three of the wolves dashed forward. One leapt for Denemir's throat. He dodged to one side, barely lifting his sword in time for it to pierce the wolf's chest. The momentum smashed Denemir against the boulder, but he held on grimly to the blade and, with his other hand, shoved at the beast. Sharp teeth snapped near his throat. He felt the wolf's hot breath before it fell and retreated, bleeding.

The second wolf was already dead on the ground, one of Talitha's arrows protruding from its eye.

The third wolf limped, its side gashed by Rannulf's axe. Rannulf, also exhausted, looked pale but angry. His grip on his axe faltered, then he caught himself. "Come on, come on!" he bellowed at the shifting wolves.

The child under the boulder wailed in terror, exciting the wolves' blood lust.

As the leader of the pack loped past, Talitha fired a shaft, catching his shoulder. The leader yelped angrily. The three remaining wolves backed off, snarling and barking at the knights. For a moment, the wolves quarreled, the bleeding wolves fighting off their healthier packmates.

"It depends on you," Denemir urged Talitha. "Else they will all charge, and rend us asunder."

She nocked, fired. A second arrow joined the first in the leader's shoulder. He howled his defiance. As Talitha reached for another arrow, the wolves gathered to swarm over her.

This is it, Denemir thought, raising a sword that weighed like lead.

Suddenly, as one, the wolves cowed in fear. They placed their tails between their legs, dropped their bellies to the earth, and whimpered. The knights stared in surprise.

Far over their heads, a man's deep voice rang out: *"Obey!"*

At the sound of the voice, two things happened. The child's wailing dropped to the gurgling hiccough of a babe trying not to cry.

And the wolves bolted into the forest.

The knights gaped in astonishment. Only bloodstains on the ground showed the wolves had ever been there.

When he recovered his wits, Denemir stepped away from the boulder, then peered at the top of it. No one was there.

Before any of them could utter a word, singing reached their ears. At that, the hiding girl stopped crying entirely.

From behind the boulder came the singer, a tall, fat man dressed in a lamb's wool coat and strange leather leggings that were of one piece with his boots. Leaves and pine needles tangled in his tousled brown hair, and mud smeared his plump cheeks. But his dark eyes sparkled so merrily, and his wordless singing lilted so sweetly, that it seemed to Denemir each tree and leaf the man passed stood higher and bloomed prouder for his passing. He carried a shepherd's crook.

The shepherd's eyes met theirs, and he looked as if he would laugh. Instead, he walked to the base of the boulder, squatted, and sang a different melody. The stinging nettles parted. The little girl crawled out from her hiding place and jumped into the shepherd's arms. Then he laughed, with such joy that the knights found themselves laughing, too.

"There you are, Slip!" he greeted the girl. He stood, lifting her. She had probably seen less than two summers. She had wispy brown baby hair and brown eyes. The child wore a thick smock of plain linen and a cloth diaper, both crusted with dirt. "Now do you see why you mustn't wander off like that?"

She hid her face in the man's shoulder and sobbed in brokenhearted relief. Tiny fists came up and knuckled her face, then tried to fit into her mouth. "There, there," he said, bouncing the toddler comfortingly. "I am here. You are safe." From a pocket, he produced a piece of sweet bread for her.

Rannulf found his voice first. "H-How did you command the wolves?"

The shepherd laughed. "I *would* command them, if they did not avoid me!"

Denemir said, "We thank you for saving our lives." Uncertainly, he decided to add a bow.

"Who are you?" asked Talitha.

The man grinned. "I am Keeper, a shepherd." He offered a hand to Denemir, who reached out to take it. The shepherd and he clasped each other by the forearm, where Denemir could feel his strength.

Keeper then clasped Talitha's forearm, and finally Rannulf's. But he did not quickly let go of Rannulf's. "Ah," the shepherd said, gazing deep into Rannulf's eyes. "The Leech of Doubt has feasted here. It will trouble you no more." As the knights watched, Rannulf's color returned to his complexion, and he stopped panting. A look of wonder crossed his face as the shepherd let go.

"And I must thank you," Keeper said, "for defending my little one until I could find her." He chuckled, and gestured at his begrimed face and hair. "I have been searching high and low. Because of you, she will live to learn from her adventure. How can I repay you? Where are you bound?"

"Castle Carousal," Denemir answered. "Do you know it? It is a fortnight's march from here."

"Indeed I do," Keeper said, adding meaningfully, "It is a good place to be *from*." He walked into the woods, singing again, a melody rich with both joy and sorrow. In his arms, Slip munched her sweet bread and hummed along happily. "Follow me!" he called cheerfully.

The knights exchanged mystified glances. Denemir shrugged, and they followed.

They pursued Keeper for a while, never quite able to catch up with him, but never losing sight nor sound of him. Denemir thought they walked a straight path all sloping uphill, though that was impossible in the forest. Despite the day's hard march and the fight, they felt strangely refreshed. Rannulf fairly skipped along.

When Keeper topped a rocky bluff, he waited for them. "An ointment for Rannulf," he sang. "A lyre for Talitha. And doves from the Citadel."

They had no idea what he meant. But when they topped the bluff, they were too startled to ask. For there, spread across the valley below them, stood Castle Carousal.

For the second time that day, the knights could only gawk. "This cannot be!" Denemir exclaimed. "Yet I grew up here; it *is* . . ."

He drank in the view, trying to comprehend. Castle Carousal's white towers climbed by the dozens, graceful and gleaming in the sunset, with triumphant pennons floating from the highest parapets. The castle's numberless stone halls rose so high, they required flying buttresses for support. The overall effect was deceptively festive and graceful, for the walls and towers were massive, thick, and had never been breached.

But the festival outside Castle Carousal dwarfed the spreading fortress. On all sides of the castle walls, at each of the gates, fairs had sprung up centuries ago. The fairs had spread and merged over the years until now they surrounded the castle and nearly filled the plain with one huge, perpetual party.

From the bluff, the booths and tents and stalls of the massive carnival formed a jumble of merry colors, with the narrow alleyways appearing as crooked lines ambling through the mess. It was undeniably the same fortress the Captain had rescued Denemir from. Even this high up, he could hear the party. The cheers and brawls and shouts and animal brayings and music merged and floated up to him as a dull roar.

"He's gone!" Talitha exclaimed.

Denemir and Rannulf whirled. Keeper had vanished. On a flat stone near where he had stood, sat a tiny bottle of blue glass; a beautiful golden lyre; and a small bird cage. Silver cloth hooded the cage.

"He did not ask our names," Rannulf marveled, "yet he knew them."

"How can these things be?" Talitha breathed.

It was then that Denemir remembered the secret chamber. *And I will be ever near, even in Ssenkrad, in guises new to you.* He laughed merrily. "Of course! It was the Captain!"

Rannulf and Talitha caught their breath. Then it hit them, too, and soon they all were laughing and pounding each other's backs and celebrating.

As Rannulf and Talitha rushed to examine their gifts, Denemir turned instead to survey sprawling Carousal. He breathed in the sweet relief of being aided and blessed by his Lord. But the remaining challenge sobered him.

Somewhere in all that decadence and temptation was one person whom the King had noticed. One person for whom he had sent Denemir.

How could he find that person?

▨ ✛ ▨

"Teller would love this," Rannulf half-shouted over the clamor, the second morning after they met Keeper. They had spent yesterday hiking to Castle Carousal and finding lodging. With their packs and gifts now safely stored at an inexpensive inn on the town's outskirts, they stood ready to search for the Captain's future soldier.

"Or despise the rivalry," Denemir answered. With his hand shielding his eyes from the morning sun, he saw two jugglers filling the air between them with countless rings; a crowd of moppets jeering the antics of violent marionettes in a puppet booth; and vendors selling every food from pastries to dark brown ale, their crowded stalls lining the dirt alley. The vendors' cries mingled with music from hand drums and recorders. Oaths and cheers burst forth nearby from a mob watching two men with quarter staves, who tried to knock each other off the log they stood upon. Denemir's nose wrinkled at every scent from roast venison to urine. Colorful pavilions snapped their tent flaps in the breeze.

The fair stretched on like this for miles.

Peasants leading an ox jostled Denemir out of the thoroughfare, without sparing him a glance. "We must divide our party," he told his friends.

A passing drunk leered at Talitha's red hair and lithe figure. He staggered over and put his arm around her waist. Calmly, she stomped her heel onto his instep. When he howled and grabbed his foot, she pushed him over. He fell to the dirt and, after a moment of struggling, passed out. A gaggle of ducks pecked at him curiously.

"Perhaps we should stick together," Rannulf hazarded.

"Then our search will take three times longer," Talitha responded. "I can protect myself. Who do we look for?"

"It is a riddle," Denemir admitted. "Here are the Captain's words: 'when you first see him, he will be sitting alone, gazing upon that which is gray yet holds all colors.'"

Rannulf sighed. "Riddles are my enemy. Know you the answer?"

Denemir said, "I have no guess. It could be some strange object one only sees at the fair. We have asked the King to bless our efforts; that must suffice."

Rannulf squared his muscular shoulders as if he were about to wrestle a bear. "'Til noon, then," he said, and plowed into the crowd.

"See you at the Lame Duck," Talitha said. She departed in another direction. In ten paces, she was lost from sight.

Denemir sighed. Picking a third direction, he began the overwhelming task.

Three hours later, head and feet aching, he had lost count of how many pavilions he had peered into. He hated the noise and hustle, which had felt so vital to him before he met the Captain.

Strange music issued from a scarlet-and-black-striped pavilion. He shouldered his way inside. Belly dancers in foreign garb danced before a raucous group of men. A man near the entrance held out an empty palm, demanding a coin for admission.

Coarse laughter exploded from the audience. One drunk, dark-haired young man had joined the dancers, imitating them clumsily and adding lewd body movements. His jacket—vivid green, with a short skirt, and the collar lined with squirrel fur—marked him as one of the wealthier peasants, who should know better. Denemir shook his head in disgust and turned to leave.

A shout stopped him. "Hoy! Gulliver, you numbnoggined sot!"

To Denemir's surprise, the obnoxious peasant was hurrying over to him. To his dismay, he suddenly recognized the man. "Adunno!" he whispered. Years of training fled from him. Suddenly feeling awkward and self-conscious, he sped his retreat.

But Adunno, clutching a stein full of ale, caught up with the knight outside. "If it isn't Gulliver the Righteous!" Adunno cried, slugging the knight in the shoulder. "Or, should I say, Gulliver the Snot-Nosed Twit? Yes, I fancy that more." The peasant grabbed the tail of Denemir's tabard and lifted it closer to his unfocused eyes. "Fresh from Evermore! How precious!" He yanked on the tabard, trying to rip it.

Denemir caught Adunno's wrist. "Greetings, Adunno," the knight said evenly. "I am now called Denemir."

"Not by me," Adunno growled, breaking his wrist free. He took a sloppy gulp of his ale, then glared at Denemir. "Put on all the holy airs you want, *knight*. To me, you are still my baby brother." He spat ale-saliva on Denemir's face.

The Captain of Despair

HALF-SHOUTING OVER the braying of livestock and the tooting of minstrel's pipes, Adunno carried on with his barrage of drunken insults. But Denemir was too busy fighting his temper to listen. Not lashing back came hard; he had more years of fighting with his brother than years of training as a knight. As he wiped the spittle from his face, he repeated inwardly, *If you fight back, you do exactly what he wants, and dishonor the King.*

A slap caught Denemir's attention sharply. "Listen to me when I speak!" Adunno ordered. "Traitor though you are, you will hear my words!"

Cheek stinging, Denemir retorted hotly, "I am no traitor!"

"No?" Adunno jeered. "You joined the army of Evermore against the wishes of our family! You left us to work the fields without you! You never write or visit!" He issued an intoxicated belch, then continued angrily, "And you have the *insolence* to tell us we displease your King! Is that not a traitor?"

A troupe of actors wearing animal masks danced by, trying to provoke fairgoers into following them to their stage.

A cow face shoved between the two men. Adunno shouted at the actor and kicked his shins, giving Denemir a moment to fumble for a reply.

Adunno's words were true, but one-sided. Before he had left, Gulliver's father and brother had done all the drinking and made Gulliver do all the field work. Besides, it was a field of *galantha*, useful only as smokeweed. "The King—" Denemir began.

" 'The King!' " Adunno mocked, energized from chasing off the actors. "The King who says no one is right except himself! Who divides families and makes brothers into enemies! Who hates for men to enjoy any pleasure!" He slurped more ale. Foam clinging to his mustache, he finished angrily, "And who does not exist! I despise your King and all he stands for! And I despise you for choosing your fantasy over your family!"

During this final speech, Denemir grew more and more angry. He took a breath to blast back at Adunno. But as his face flushed with rage, he saw his brother break into a satisfied grin. Just in time, Denemir realized he was about to play into Adunno's hands, and he forced himself to calm down. His Captain, in a similar situation, had not defended himself. Quietly, Denemir asked, "How wise is it to despise Someone you have never met?"

Adunno growled and drew back his stein, to dash the ale in Denemir's face. When Denemir neither flinched nor raised a hand, Adunno looked confused. Finally, muttering, "Waste of perfectly good ale," he turned and tottered away, into the belly dancers' tent.

Denemir wilted. Two mimes in front of a pastry cart began mockingly imitating the encounter between Denemir and Adunno, but the knight ignored them. Facing his brother had taken more out of him than any physical combat in recent memory.

And he was no closer to finding the person the Captain had sent him for.

◈ ✝ ◈

Rannulf and Talitha had no more luck finding the Captain's quarry than Denemir had. As the days passed, they continued searching the fair, then returning to the Lame Duck each night, a tired and footsore trio. Denemir, embarrassed by both his brother's words and deeds, did not tell the others of finding Adunno. They could see he was depressed, but assumed it was because they had not yet finished their mission.

On the fifth night, as every night, they went over the Captain's words again. Red hair glistening in the room's candlelight, Talitha repeated, "What is gray, yet holds all colors?"

Slumped on a wooden chair too small for him, Rannulf bumped his forehead lightly with his mace, over and over, as if coaxing an answer from his brain. The silence dragged on.

Sheathing a freshly polished blade, Denemir suggested, "If we list things that are gray, that may lead us to an answer."

"Agreed," Talitha commended. She found some parchment and a quill pen, and the knights began dictating a list.

Squirrel. Wool. Steel. Ash. Hair. Pot.

"A pot could be gray, but hold all colors," Talitha observed. "If there were paints in it."

Rannulf looked glum. "In the last five days, I have seen over six score people holding pots."

The other two sighed heavily.

Clay. Stone. Castle. Clouds. Fog. Cat. Horse.

When they grew too sleepy to continue, Rannulf concluded, "If we find someone holding fog in one hand and a horse in the other, we have our man."

"But he must be sitting on a fallen pine," Denemir mumbled.

Talitha snapped out of her drowsiness. "What?"

A wave of embarrassment swept over Denemir. "I forgot 'til now!" he confessed. "The Captain said he would be 'sitting alone, on a fallen pine, gazing upon that which is gray yet holds all colors.'"

"That changes everything," Rannulf said. "There are no fallen pines in the fair."

"But there are fallen pines around the edge of the fair, where they are clearing the forest to make the fair larger!" Talitha exclaimed.

"And if he is at the edge of the fair, he is more likely to be sitting alone!" Talitha added triumphantly.

"Then we will find him tomorrow!" Rannulf stated. The three knights stared at each other, eyes bright with hope for the first time in many days.

✙

Finding someone on the forested edge of the fair sounded easy. But after hours of tramping in the hot sun, Denemir now realized how many miles it was around the everlasting party.

Sweating, feet aching, he searched for a shady place to sit and catch his breath. Up a grassy slope, he spied a wedged mass of pines that the carpenters had felled, but the laborers had not yet dragged away. Even lying sideways, some of the huge trees poked branches skyward far enough to provide shade. He hiked amidst the tangled trunks and plopped down on one of them, under dappled shadows.

He sighed and rubbed his painful feet. After a few moments of rest, he knew he should move on, but he could hardly force himself. It had been five days of frustration. What was the use of going on? Yet he must.

Mired in conflicting thoughts, Denemir gradually realized that he was not alone among the toppled pines. Jutting pine branches blocked much of his view, but he could discern another young man sitting lost in thought, fifty feet directly ahead of him.

The young man sat half in and half out of the shade. Shadows covered his face and shoulders, but Denemir could discern a new beard in progress and, on what he could see of the young man's face, a rare expression.

Sometimes in the Citadel, Denemir had known young men and women betrothed but not yet wed. They had a way of staring into one another's eyes with such naked love that he felt compelled to look away. Strangers were not meant to witness the intimacies they displayed openly on their faces.

The look on the young man's face was of that kind. Not love, but wonder. And longing.

Sunlight illuminated his brown leggings and boots, plus the object of his concentration, held in his lap: a plain gray pigeon feather. The young man held the feather by its stem and idly twisted it. As it spun between his fingers, it caught the sunlight, broke it, and threw it at Denemir's eyes.

The sun reflected off the shiny feather in all the colors of the prism.

Denemir stifled a gasp.

He stared again at the young man's face. Branches obscured almost all but the eyes, yet they were enough. He knew he had never seen inside anyone's heart like this. He felt he should look away, but he couldn't. It was like seeing, really seeing, someone down deep for the first time.

And the thoughts of this young man's heart were: *This miraculous feather is strong enough to propel the bird, yet light enough not to encumber. It can slice the air or rest upon it. It can repel water. And, in sunlight, this plain feather becomes a work of art. It is surely no accident. I long to know its Creator . . . but Who, and how?*

Transfixed, Denemir stood. "The King saw your heart," he whispered. "It is for you I have come. Through Despair's Pit, despite the Leech of Doubt." Oblivious of the broken branches and trunks, he began walking toward the man holding the feather. "Braving the soldiers of Ssenkrad, shunning Teller's distractions," Denemir went on, "defying wolves, and searching through the rabble day after day . . ."

He stood directly in front of the young man, who only now noticed him. Denemir finished, "It is for you I have come."

The young man looked up. His expression changed from wonder to irritation.

Without distance and branches in the way, Denemir recognized him, even beneath the new beard. The marvelous feeling of seeing anew shattered.

It was Adunno, his brother.

"Then you have wasted your journey," Adunno retorted. Dashing the feather to the ground, he rose. "I told you my piece, and I will hear nothing from you. Do not turn yourself into a nuisance." Without a glance back, he strode down the hill, back into the revelry.

Denemir whispered in woe, "This cannot be! The King is mistaken!" He cried, "Adunno *cannot* be the one I was sent for! He does not want to hear of Evermore! Least of all from me!"

But his heart knew the King did not make mistakes.

He backed away from the spot where Adunno had sat. The mission had suddenly become impossible, and all his good intentions turned into naive idealism. He had been tricked. He wanted to bolt, to run someplace where there were no problems, no need to believe against all odds. He

182 + Scott & Renee Pinzon

turned, vaulted over a massive pine trunk, and fled down the grassy slope.

From behind the last clump of pine branches, a huge dark figure stepped into view. Ebony armor soaked up the sunlight without returning it. Icy vapor curled out of its black visor. Dried blood crusted the spikes on its shoulders and gauntlets. Cold, mocking laughter from the pit echoed out of its helmet. "Did I not tell you," the Captain of Despair rasped, "that I would return when you were less vigilant?"

Denemir tried to draw his sword and stop his downhill flight at the same time. Instead, his feet slipped on the dew-moistened grass. He fell on his back and skidded part way down the slope.

Despair leaped to the attack. He straddled the flailing Denemir, batwings blocking the sun, and drove his freezing blade down.

Denemir's wild parry barely knocked the blade to one side; it drove deep into the sod near his ribs. While Despair struggled to yank his blade out of the earth, the knight tucked his knees up to his chest and executed a backwards somersault. He regained his footing and took a defensive stance as Despair freed the blade.

The Captain of Despair lifted one taloned hand and pointed at Denemir. In a hoarse imitation of the knight's voice, Despair mocked, "It is for you I have come."

Denemir's eyes searched desperately for help. The fair, far down the slope, presented only the backs of pavilions and stalls. He could see nothing of the people inside them.

He was alone. His left arm tensed reflexively, and he suddenly noted that his shield was gone. He had dropped it near the log where Adunno sat,.

Despair advanced, chanting his familiar litany. "I never tire. I never give in. I am more patient than you. I am older than you. I am stronger than you . . ."

With each sentence, Despair advanced a step and Denemir retreated a step. Then the knight felt one of the fallen tree trunks prod his back. He could not retreat.

Icy waves emanated from the Captain of Despair, washing over Denemir. The knight swung the sword weakly, with no specific target in mind.

Despair parried the feeble blow. His ebony blade darted in and touched Denemir's left thigh.

Instantly, the knight's entire leg turned numb. Denemir cried out. He shifted his weight to his right leg. For a moment, the wound adrenalized him, and he flailed at Despair, raining blows upon the black armor.

Despair waited until Denemir had spent his energy. With ease, the dark opponent slipped his cold blade through the knight's defenses and stabbed the other leg.

All of Denemir's support turned numb. Unable to feel or move his legs, he collapsed to his knees before the Captain of Despair. "Yessss," Despair breathed out in wintry vapors. "Much better."

Gasping, fighting tears, Denemir raised his sword.

Despair gloated. He engaged Denemir's blade with a circular thrusting motion and flicked it out of the knight's hand.

"I make you a promisssse," Despair hissed.

Weaponless, terrified, yet still defiant, Denemir stammered, "Y-your promises are worthless."

"I promise I will not kill you," Despair said.

Something in the way he said it sent a thrill of terror through Denemir.

Then came the ebony blade, and the sensation of a glacier exploding in Denemir's heart.

◼ ✛ ◼

In the darkness, a single red candle created a tiny circle of light. The circle revealed part of a scarred wooden table and a single sheet of parchment. Holding a quill pen, the hand which had filled most of the parchment with shaky letters paused. The parchment said:

> *O Captain,*
>
> *I have found Adunno but he will not talk to me. I try but he hates us both. Thus I do not know how to show him your glory.*
>
> *The Captain of Despair wounds me sorely each day. Rannulf removes the pain using the oil you gave him. Then on the morrow Despair torments me again. I have lost my shield and dulled my sword. He never tires. He never gives in. I am powerless against him.*
>
> *Request that you relieve me of this mission. I have failed you.*

The hand waited, suspended, as the author reread the parchment. Then the hand signed a name at the end: *"Gulliver."* There was a choked sob, and a single tear landed on the parchment, smearing the name.

The hand blotted the parchment, then folded it and rolled it into a tiny tube.

Another hand moved the candle. The circle of light swept over the table to reveal a cage, covered with a silver hood. The hands lifted the hood, opened the cage, and withdrew a white dove.

The dove had a tiny wooden canister attached to its leg. The hands opened it, tucked the parchment inside, and replaced the cap.

A *scrunch*: the chair pushed away from the table.

A footfall.

A *creak*: the shutters opened to reveal a cold, starry night.

A flap and flutter: the dove escaped the hands and soared into the night clouds.

A whisper: "To the Citadel, feathered champion."

A long, long wait.

15

Secrets Seen in the Sword

I T IS his habit to play near here each day," Denemir wearily informed Talitha and Rannulf. His muscles ached from too many duels with Despair. His leg wounds forced him to limp. His bruises noted each bump and prod from the milling crowd, as the knights stood on a low rise and peered across miles of medieval fair.

Booths of merchants selling food, exotic spices, imported fabrics, and palm-read fortunes lined the narrow lane ahead of them. Nearby, under a large, open-sided tent, a crowd laughed at a vulgar play while indulging in ale and brandy. Behind the tent, those who had overindulged sprawled unconscious in the mud, or collapsed to hands and knees, puking.

"There he is," Denemir noted. He pointed down the lane, toward six or seven knaves seated at a table under a small pavilion, gaming with dice. They were too far away to hear, but the knights could see them clearly.

"Which is Adunno?" Rannulf asked. "I would see the one for whom I have faced such hardship."

"In the scarlet jacket," Denemir replied. "His beard new."

Adunno, gloating, stretched his arms over the table to rake in a pile of coins, as Rannulf eyed the gamblers. "Quite the peacock," he commented. "Why does he despise the King so, since the King has sent us all this way for him?"

"It escapes me," Denemir confessed, "though I fear it is somehow my fault."

As they spoke, one of the gamblers, a brawny blonde farmer's son, grabbed Adunno's arm in a *not-so-fast* gesture. Adunno shrugged the hand away, making a sharp comment.

"The Captain told you this man is ready to hear of Evermore?" Talitha puzzled. "Therefore, why will he not?"

"'Tis a mystery," Denemir admitted. "For I once saw the longing on his face."

Just then Adunno and the strapping blonde jumped up, quarreling. They stood chest to chest, shoving each other in turn. The other men leaped to their feet and took sides, shouting.

"'Ware the man in blue," Rannulf rumbled. His hand traveled instinctively to the Morning Star at his belt.

One of the gamblers, a man sporting a blue waistcoat, unsheathed a dagger, hiding it behind his hip. He sidled around the squabbling group, seeking a way to reach Adunno.

Talitha gasped. "We must protect him!" she cried. "The King loves him!"

Denemir's sword rang and glittered as he drew it. The knights surged forward through the crowd. Just then, a butcher's helper herded several lowing cows through the narrow thoroughfare, blocking all traffic. "No!" Denemir shouted.

The knights watched helplessly as Adunno, angered, hurled the dice at the farmer's son. The huge blonde reddened, then smashed Adunno in the face. Three of the gamblers jumped on the blonde, driving him to the ground, as Adunno fell against the support stake. The pavilion collapsed, smothering the combatants under green canvas.

"Hoy!" Rannulf bellowed at the cows. "Move!" He swatted the nearest one, which sped up for two whole steps.

Lumps under the canvas rose, fell, slid violently. Then two of the gamblers crawled out from under it and fled. Two more followed, running in opposite directions. Finally the muscular blonde wriggled out from under the canvas. His pockets bulged. He turned and helped the man in blue to his feet. They fled together.

The knights pushed past the last cow and dashed to the collapsed tent. Talitha and Rannulf ran to opposite sides, grabbed the edge of the canvas, and threw it back like a large bedcover.

There lay Adunno, dazed, his head squarely against the stout tent stake. A light slash across his cheek and a deep cut in his left shoulder oozed blood.

Denemir knelt, still holding the Sword of the Spirit in one hand. He slipped his other arm beneath his brother's shoulders and lifted him to a sitting position.

Adunno shook his head to clear it, then let out a low

groan and gingerly touched the back of his head. He blinked in the sunlight. Shakily, he stood.

Denemir glanced at his sword, looking for a one-handed way to sheathe it, and inhaled sharply. Eyes wide, Denemir stared up at the groggy Adunno, then back at the sword. "By the Citadel!" he exclaimed. "Here is the problem! Talitha! Rannulf! Look into the Sword!"

The other two gathered around and gasped. Rannulf reached out and felt the air over Adunno's shoulder, then stared back at the Sword.

Reflected in the polished blade, there stood Adunno, cautiously touching the cut on his face. And with him, they could see three additional creatures.

One looked like the smaller brother of the Captain of Despair. It stood behind Adunno, black as blindness, ugly as dried blood, strong as rebellion. His gauntleted hands covered Adunno's eyes.

The second and third creatures flanked Adunno, whispering in the young man's ears. They had hind legs like lizards, arms and hands like humans, and faces like lionesses. Hatred and suspicion lit their cat-shaped eyes, which darted back and forth warily.

But when Denemir looked at his older brother without aid of the sword, everything appeared normal. The beasts were invisible and intangible.

"Adunno," Denemir urged. "Your mind is not your own! Awake!" He gazed into the Sword of the Spirit. He saw the lionesses glare at him and snarl. Each one poked a talon into

Adunno's ears, deafening him in case Denemir continued his pleas. The black, armored beast stood impassively, hands covering Adunno's eyes.

"The mystery is revealed," Talitha said. "We struggle not against flesh and blood!"

Now Adunno had recovered. He glared at Talitha and Rannulf. When he saw Denemir, he reddened. "Traitor!" he said. His gaze fell upon the gaming table. All the coins had vanished. "Come to rob me while I was stunned, dint you?"

"Nay! The gold-haired villein—" Denemir began.

"Waste not your breath, you pestilence!" Adunno spat. "Fair warning: if you approach me again, I shall stab you!"

Denemir sighed heavily. "Listen once more to but six words, Adunno. Then until you ask me the rest of the message, I will not trouble you." He regarded Adunno with profound sadness. "Here they are: The King of Evermore loves you." The reflection in the sword showed the lionesses snarling and clawing in his direction as they plugged Adunno's ears.

Adunno blinked once, as if stabbed again. Then, cradling his wounded arm, he stalked away. The three beasts matched him stride for stride, the catlizards whispering rapidly in his ears, shooting dirty looks at Denemir.

Rannulf, resting his fists on his hips, stared after them. "Had he stayed another moment, I would have tested my mace on those creatures," he grumbled.

"You would have accomplished nothing, except to frighten Adunno," Talitha replied. "He is entirely unaware of them."

Several paces away, Denemir exclaimed, "Captain, have mercy!" In the middle of the lane, he hobbled in a slow circle, staring aghast into the Sword of the Spirit.

Though invisible to the mortal eye, the creatures were everywhere. Almost every fairgoer in the crowd had one whispering to her, or blinding him, or perched on her back, or helping him lift a jug of stout to his lips. They clustered in crowds around the fortune teller's booths, squatting over the entrance like vultures waiting to feast on carrion.

All of them menacing. All of them ugly. Saliva glistening from all their fangs. Hate glaring from all their eyes, which were trained upon the three knights.

◈ ✟ ◈

Denemir signed the parchment, rolled it into a small, tight tube, and sealed it. He rose from the table, reached past the golden lyre Keeper had given Talitha, and opened the silver-hooded cage. He stooped and peered inside. Gratefulness filled his heart. "There are still two," he marveled.

He gently withdrew a dove from the cage, and closed the small door. He tucked his message into a tiny tube attached to the dove's leg, then capped the tube.

Limping to the open second-story window, he released the dove. It beat high into a cloudless sky, circled once, then soared away toward the Citadel.

He turned and sat on the window sill. "There are still two," he told his friends. "Days have turned into weeks, and

I have sent a message to the King or the Captain every day. Yet each morning when I open the cage, there are two doves there again. This is a most gracious enchantment."

"Then he has not entirely forgotten us," Rannulf said. He chewed a drumstick gloomily, then added, "Though, if not, why does his answer delay so?"

Talitha picked up the golden lyre and let her fingers idly play over the strings. Harp-like chords thrummed in the room. Her face was sober and thinner. They had all lost weight as the weeks wore on. "Despair has bested each of us more than once. We cannot leave the room without being forced into mortal combat. Our only salvation has been that he has not beat all of us on the same day. That, and the anointing oil Keeper gave Rannulf to soothe our wounds. But my fear is . . . unless the King answers soon . . ." A lump rose in her throat, and she swallowed it down. "How much longer can we live like this?"

Denemir rose stiffly from the window sill. Pushing back the pain, he answered, "My heart longs to leave here. I miss the Citadel more than life itself. And yet . . . and yet, I will not quit until the Captain relieves me of this burden." He drew his sword slowly, and contemplated it. His muscles ached when he lifted it. It seemed much duller than it had been when the journey began. Chinks spoiled the edge. It showed as much wear as his torn tabard.

He closed his eyes, fighting a headache, and said quietly, "This is *my* mission, which your love has compelled you to take upon yourselves. You have done far more than I would ask. Know that you may leave whenever you desire. But as for me . . . "

He opened his eyes. Sadness still filled them, but now resolve lived there, too. He finished, "Though He slay me, yet will I trust Him."

◈ ✝ ◈

On the seventieth day of waiting, Denemir was composing another desperate letter to his Captain when Talitha said, "There is a wind stirring in the trees."

Rannulf met her at the high window. Far away, across the fair, rose the mighty pines where Denemir had watched Adunno study the pigeon feather. A stiff breeze from Evermore grew into a hard wind, until the pines rocked. Still the wind grew. "Denemir," Rannulf called. "This is no ordinary wind."

Denemir joined them at the window. The hundred-foot pines bent as the gale roared over. Yet the air over the fair remained strangely calm. Oblivious, the fairgoers partied on.

Rannulf reached over and unsheathed Denemir's sword. Turning his back to the window, he held the blade so it reflected what was outside. He cried, "The King's answer!"

At that moment their eyes were opened, and behold, a rushing army of flying warriors sped from Evermore, pennants streaming and swords bared. Wind and clouds fled from their wings of power. In an endless stream, they poured over the trees into the air over Castle Carousal. And the dread creatures of the fair rose from the ground to meet them, forming rank upon rank in the sky.

The sword clattered to the floor from Rannulf's heedless fingers. The knights stared, transfixed, at the King's supernatural might.

Some of the flying warriors resembled beautiful young men and women, muscular and golden. Others resembled beasts, fierce and scarred and born for battle. Some shone so brightly, the knights could not discern their shape. But each bore arms and each blazed with power. As the hundreds of beings hovered and formed columns over the fair, their gaze upon the forces of evil was grim and terrible.

Despair flapped heavily up from the heart of the fair, and rose to the front of the evil army. Several Captains joined him, even larger and more appalling. Finally, the largest creature of all, tall as three men, glided on dark wings to the front lines and hovered, waiting. He roared his defiance. When he opened his black maw, Denemir saw into it.

As the ocean surges into the mouth of a whale, everything seemed to pour into that greedy mouth, even light itself. Denemir felt the presence of a bottomless pit, fed by unquenchable desire. Then he realized that this was Lust, the Ruler of the Fair.

"Look at the people!" Talitha exclaimed.

Denemir tore his eyes from the sky and looked below.

Everything appeared perfectly normal. Gamblers gambled, sellers sold, dancers danced, drinkers drank. All were completely unaware of the battle forming overhead.

The last golden warriors arrived. The wind abated.

Throngs jammed the sky over the fair. Each army had formed its lines and columns. At the front of Evermore's army floated a strong and shining winged man in brilliant silver armor; and next to him, a warrior bearing a golden horn. Unafraid, they faced Lust and his dread Captains and their legions.

And waited.

And waited.

"Why do they delay?" Talitha cried.

"Strike!" urged Rannulf. "Avenge the King!"

Still the armies waited.

The sun crossed the sky. Morning shadows shrank, vanished.

Afternoon shadows grew. The fair partied on. But the knights and the rest of the world held their breath.

16
Return to the Secret Chamber

AT LAST Denemir spoke. "Evermore's army awaits a signal," he proposed. "And Ssenkrad's army dares not relax its guard. Stalemate, unless we discover the signal!"

Suddenly Talitha laughed with the joy of discovery. She plucked up her lyre and climbed out the window. Mystified, Denemir and Rannulf watched her clamber out of sight, upwards.

From above, her head poked into sight, upside down. "Come!" she grinned. "To the roof!"

They found her leaning against the inn's stone chimney. As they joined her, she plucked the golden lyre. The chord sent a ripple through the ranks of Evermore. In a clear, sweet voice, she sang,

> *Clap your hands, all you nations;*
> *Shout to the King with cries of joy.*
> *How awesome is our Lord Most High;*
> *The great King will our foes destroy!*

Denemir and Rannulf recognized the battle song, and joined in enthusiastically:

He puts the nations under us,
The world under our feet.
He ascends, 'mid shouts of joy;
Sound the trumpets, and repeat:

Sing praises to the King, sing praises;
Sing praises to our King, sing praises!

Although Talitha's voice was pleasant, Denemir's tenor was average at best, and Rannulf's baritone barely changed notes no matter where the song went. The men felt foolish, singing on the inn's roof in the face of war. But praises for the King marshaled powerful forces beyond the music. As the knights worshipped, the shining warriors roared cheers, and the dark warriors screamed frustration. When the knights reached the chorus, the warrior with the horn blew a single piercing note. Evermore's army threw itself at its enemies.

The knights sang and watched. Dozens of dark beings plummeted from the sky with mortal wounds. Within minutes, Lust and his Captains fled, so full of holy javelins they resembled pin cushions. The evil army fell into disarray, and Evermore's warriors swept over them like a flood.

Laughing, celebrating, the knights took to the cobblestone streets. They stopped the first people they encountered, a group of teens about to enter a tavern. "We bring tidings from Evermore," Denemir smiled. "Do you know our King?"

The leader of the group looked amazed. "This is luck most fair," he said. "Just today I began longing to know of Evermore. I will hear you gladly."

Everywhere they went, the reaction was the same. Without creatures to blind and deafen them, the people received the King's love with joy.

Now, instead of spending all day traipsing through the fair searching for Adunno, the knights spoke to everyone they met. They held meetings at some of the fair's stages, and hundreds turned from drinking and gaming to come.

Nearly a week later, on his way to one such meeting, Denemir chanced upon Adunno, who was purchasing scarlet cloth to replace his ruined jacket.

Denemir steeled himself for the torrent of abuse.

But Adunno, arm in a sling, stood meekly before his younger brother. He said, "I have been searching for you." Then he stared at his own boots.

"I have not pestered you," Denemir said.

Adunno cracked a rueful smile. "And I no longer desire to stab you. Somehow I see things differently these days. I have thought much on how I treated you, and how you never lashed back at me. I begin to realize how dear to you your King must be, that you would leave family and suffer abuse for Him, and still remain faithful."

Denemir waited until Adunno glanced up. Looking straight into his eyes, Denemir said, "He has sent me for you."

Adunno swallowed. "So say you." He glanced around

for a moment, then summoned the courage to meet Denemir's gaze. "Then . . . what is the rest of His message to me?"

At that moment, most of Denemir's bruises, aches, and pains miraculously diminished. Denemir beamed. "Come to Evermore," he invited. "Let Him tell it to you Himself."

◈ ✛ ◈

In the pre-dawn twilight, the mist from the falls chilled the knight's face and hands. Drops gathered in his uncut brown hair, and on the links of his chain mail; but it would take much more than cold to keep him from his secret meeting. He pushed through the brambles and wild ivy beside the stream to hidden stone stairs, cut into the mountain beside the falls, and limped up them.

The stairs ended in a secret chamber of rock, etched centuries ago by the flow of the Crystal Stream, and now hidden behind a curtain of water. For the entire eastern wall of the alcove opened to show the back of the waterfall. The splash of the water cascading into the stream below echoed in the room, which smelled of wet stone.

The Captain of the Host stood waiting before the waterfall. As his steely eyes fell upon the knight, a warm smile spread across his face. The strong Captain Prince crossed the room in two strides and crushed the knight to his chest in a long, heartfelt embrace.

Then the knight sank to his knees, bowing his head. "We have accomplished your mission, my Lord. And we have brought you prisoners from Ssenkrad."

The Captain smiled upon him. "Well done, my good and faithful servant. Arise." As the knight stood, the Captain put an arm around his shoulder. "I know you have many questions. I will answer them all—some now, the rest much later. But first, show me the captives."

They walked together into the waterfall, which parted itself around them. Still dry, they stepped out onto a ledge that overlooked the valley. Rannulf, Talitha, Adunno, and over three hundred Ssenkradians knelt in the grass, awaiting the Captain's bidding.

He looked upon them and chuckled, then pounded Denemir's shoulder. "Though I know such victory is not bought cheaply," the Captain said, "it brings me great joy when you take prisoners."

At that moment, the dawn sun peeked over the hills, pouring a golden bath into the valley. Butterflies swarmed to greet the dawn. The light of a thousand sunrises shone in the Captain's eyes. "It is worth our sacrifices," he said, "to set them free."

✝ ✝ ✝

About the Authors

Though Scott and Renee Pinzon have collaborated on numerous published short stories, this is their first book together.

Scott Pinzon sold his first short story at age 15. Except for a short detour during his late teens to play in a folk rock band, he has been writing fiction ever since. He authored two young adult novels before *Knights of Evermore*. He is also an award-winning marketing communications writer.

Renee Pinzon was Dopey when Scott first met her. (Her job at Disneyland required her at various times to portray each of the Seven Dwarves.) She was just Scott's type. The two have been married twenty years.

The Pinzons are active as worship leaders and musicians at Northwest Community Church. They live with their two teenagers in the upper left corner of the United States, where the main mission of the church is to convince the locals that espresso is not a religion (although it may be a valid art form). If you write them a letter in care of the publisher, they promise an astoundingly slow response.